Chantal Pelletier, born in Lyon, began her career as a theatre actor. She founded a theatre company in Paris and is a successful author of novels, essays, plays and film scripts. It is not unusual to find her engaged simultaneously as author, director and actor in the same project. She published her first *roman noir* in 1997. In *Goat Song* she introduces Maurice Laice, the world-weary inspector of three of her crime novels. *Goat Song* won the Grand Prix du roman noir of Cognac in 2001.

GOAT SONG

Chantal Pelletier

Translated from the French by Ian Monk

BITTER LEMON PRESS
LONDON

BITTER LEMON PRESS

First published in the United Kingdom in 2004 by
Bitter Lemon Press, 37 Arundel Gardens, London W11 2LW

www.bitterlemonpress.com

First published in French as *Le Chant du Bouc* by
Éditions Gallimard. Paris 2000

This book is supported by the French Ministry for
Foreign Affairs, as part of the Burgess programme
administered by the Institut Français
du Royaume-Uni on behalf of the French
Embassy in London and by the French
Ministry of Culture (Centre National du Livre);
publié avec le concours du Ministère des
Affaires Etrangères (Programme Burgess) et du
Ministère de La Culture (Centre National du Livre)

A CIP record for this book is available from the British Library

ISBN 1–904738–03–6

Typeset by RefineCatch Limited, Broad Street, Bungay, Suffolk
Printed and bound in Great Britain by Bookmarque Ltd,
Croydon, Surrey

For HM

"Sorry?"
"Men like you are always sorry, and always too late!"
Marianne to Ferdinand in Jean-Luc Godard's
Pierrot le Fou

A cold stench of sweat, tobacco, saltpetre, whiffs of bleach and ammonia. Elsa crossed the entrance hall of the Moulin Rouge without greeting the cleaning ladies. At ten o'clock in the morning, the music hall that had set the legendary heart of Montmartre beating, where Lautrec and Picasso kicked up their heels and caught the clap, was no postcard. The girl in the red raincoat burst into the office of the imbecilic personnel manager, whose mouth was constantly agape from stupidity and chronic sinusitis.

"Rose is leaving. I want to take her place with the two lead dancers."

"Um, uh . . ."

"I want to become a dresser. Rose'll teach me. That way, you won't have to train up anyone. The director agrees. And so does the stage manager. I've asked them."

"So we'll be losing another pain in the arse from the sewing room. Great!"

"I'll be good. I promise!"

She yelled out a thank you then ran up the spiral staircase towards the door of the men's dressing rooms to tell Manfred that she'd soon be taking care of him every evening. By clothing her darling, she'd manage to seduce him with her hands and eyes.

Behind the door, Manu Chao was belting out *je ne t'aime plus mon amour, je ne t'aime plus tous les jours*. She knocked. Manfred didn't answer. She opened the door and found herself face to face with a rail full of costumes that was barring her way. She pushed it slightly aside, making its wheels grate menacingly. Then Elsa saw her love swimming in his blood. She didn't have time to scream.

Hot blood is flowing down her throat, slithering over her lips, spilling its body heat onto the clay floor. A sweet smell fills her skull, her eyes close to embrace death. In the darkness of her eyelids, screams from men ring out as they are shot down like dogs, the raucous rattle of the Kalashnikovs, the whistle of bullets and the dull, almost soft sound of metal penetrating the flesh of men, women and the tender muscles of children. Blood of her blood stains her skin. Close your eyes. Stay still. Death protects us from everything.

Maurice Laice shrank back, as though he'd disturbed a couple making love. But it was just death. Love and death again. The corpses piled one on the other, mingling their blood, looked as if they'd been punished for a forbidden union. The resulting still life could have been entitled *Storm of Blood in a Bijou Residence*. Those gaping arteries had sprayed the mirrors, powder, make-up and spangles. Slaughters like this one really didn't go with such brightly coloured curtains, or the pale carpet, which had presumably once been pink, though Maurice couldn't swear to it. Fortunately, the patches of gore seemed to be the same colour as fallen maple leaves. Being colour-blind wasn't all bad! He unwrapped a stick of cinnamon-flavoured chewing gum and folded it into his mouth. Having to face such carnage on the way back from his father's funeral was a bit more than he could take. It was almost enough to make him feel queasy.

Unsticking those two bodies that were glued together with coagulated blood was not going to be fun. Why did Maurice imagine such things? Maybe because of his mother, who he'd just left out there in a village near Mâcon, alone with a dead man who would continue to linger in her household routines for years. How to cast off your other half after forty-two years of marriage? On being separated, that flesh which had been grafted together must peel away, just as it would for these two butchered specimens who were about to be split. At that moment, Maurice's own blood drained from his skull. He leaned against the doorjamb, tracing a line of haemoglobin down his coat as he did so. His heart was beating like mad. He tried to calm himself down by remembering how he, at least, was glued to no one. He had all his own flesh, just to himself, and one day his coffin would swallow up a sack of old, but totally intact skin.

The youth and beauty of the two victims were terrible to behold. Their dark eyes gleamed like polished pebbles in the snow. Maurice kneeled down, just stopping himself from touching the girl's icy cheek. Legs straight out of a commercial, in hold-up stockings, emerged from her scarlet raincoat. Her transparent face, topped by black hair, could have belonged to one of those baby-faced virgins on the ceiling of the Sistine Chapel. A Michelangelo angel. Momo's heart was sprouting wings. Already, back at Granville, he had been smitten by a lovely holidaymaker, murdered in her seaweed bath. It made him wonder if he was becoming a necrophile. His eyes turned to the naked, solidly muscular body of the man, his brown hair curling around his face, with its thick sensuous mouth. It was easy to see why jerks from Tokyo or Cincinnati came in droves to admire his grace among the dancing girls. Momo stood up, waiting for his head to stop spinning.

"My deepest sympathy, Inspector," said a cop who had shown up in a sweat, a large camera bouncing on his belly.

Maurice sketched a mournful smile around his cigarillo. This idiot was talking about his father in front of this horror show. He could shove his sympathy up his arse. Why couldn't all these shit-heads go and dump their fine words elsewhere?

"I didn't know them personally," Maurice said, straight-faced. "As for my father, thanks."

No one could sympathize with his grief. And was it even grief? More like a chill. His father's death opened the door on the black hole waiting for him, and a blast of cold air was now freezing his bones. He had been warned. He was now to be head of the queue at the door separating him from the next world. As for this butchered couple here, they must have been taken by surprise. There were presumably loads of people holding open the door for them and saying: "Don't worry, so long as I'm here, you've nothing to fear. I'll go before you do."

The personnel manager arrived, mouth agape. Maurice wasn't quite sure why he found this character so irritating.

"And no one heard anything?"

"There was music playing full blast, and no one else in the dressing rooms. Only Manfred was due to rehearse, because of a change of partners."

Momo looked at him. That's what was bugging him: the way he breathed with his mouth open, completely oblivious to how useful a nose can be.

In the gory bijou dressing room the fat sweaty cop was flashing his camera at the loving couple. Maurice thought fleetingly how much the girl looked like the only woman he'd ever dared keep by his side for any length of time. But that now seemed so long ago. Back then, he'd still believed in happiness. Ever since, he'd stopped himself from thinking about her. Memories of her plunged him into an ocean of blues, and he didn't have sea legs.

He bent down over a dog-eared photo stuck on the mirror above the dressing table. Blood had pock-marked its background, but the portrait was still perfectly visible. But Maurice was unsure if it was a man, woman, a girlfriend or a mother. The person looked ageless and sexless. He picked it up with his handkerchief.

The boys from forensics appeared. Maurice went out to make room for them. There wasn't enough space in Montmartre to play cowboys and indians.

"Try and be precise for once. Because we're going to have to stage the scene that led up to this final tableau. To work out who was the intended victim. Him, her, or both of them."

"She wanted to become a dresser," the personnel manager announced. "And I didn't say no. She'd been working for the last eighteen months in the sewing room. She made costumes, she dreamed of becoming a fashion designer . . ."

Momo saw the boys get out their magnifying glasses and brushes, producing the strange effect of cleaning off make-up in this music hall dressing room, a curious version of the order of things. In other words, the usual shit-heap. He went with Gaping Mouth to his office. Manfred Godalier had been taken on as a lead dancer six months back. He was twenty-nine, born in the Somme department. As for Elsa Suppini, she was twenty-one, and from Bastia, Corsica.

A Corsican from Bastia, for Momo, was like lemon juice on a live oyster. He had no desire to get himself caught up in a worse than Cretan labyrinth, with cretins in hoods out to have your balls for breakfast. But this was no time to think testicles. Momo preferred to ignore their existence. Anything to do with sex turned him off. One day, that little ball-breaker Agnes had come out with the following complaint: "The closer you get to being a stiff, the less stiff you get." The fucking cow! Not everyone's born misogynous, but

8

some women seem to work hard at keeping it up as a tradition. Agnes was so far off her trolley that Maurice had been though his own personal Waterloo and still hadn't got over it. The main occupant of his Y-fronts had stayed as limp as cotton. Total calm. Any quieter, and you'd be dead. He still resented the fact that this lover of shiatsu and Zen hadn't been more encouraging. Whatever people say, a man needs a helping hand sometimes, not a constant put-down. He'd dared to utter a meek "You're so hard!", which had been volleyed straight back with a "And you're not!" One laugh too many and a backhanded insult meant that a forty-something, rather fragile individual had lost it, and any hope of getting it back. Just before his father's death, when his mother had called – "Come quick, your father's very ill" – Maurice had torn up his invitation to Agnes's wedding. But this hadn't been bad news. More like a relief really, because the crazy bitch had regularly come and strutted around him, like a she-cat in heat in front of a tom. In the end, when cats screw, it's because the females are burning up, and the males relieve themselves. But neither of them is really involved. They prefer scratching and pissing on walls so as to say "My patch, keep off". Over the years, Maurice Laice hadn't even managed to make his walls stink bad enough to stop the spread of murders in his manor. He always got there too late, to catch the reflection of a killer in the eyes of a corpse.

When he went back into the dressing room, he took a long hard look at the face of the twenty-one-year-old Corsican girl. Elsa Suppini. In her eyes Momo thought he could read fear, incomprehension, the sorrow of someone who had too much will to die so soon. But there was no hatred. Maurice felt a frisson rise up his

9

back. He knew that when he was confronted with the murderer, he would be gripped by infinite sadness and despair.

"You really need guts to become a dresser. They get fired almost as easily as the dancing girls!"

Maurice pulled his coat over his chest. It was freezing in this damp workroom with its two feeble oil heaters.

"So they often sack dancers?"

"They come here from Poland, or Russia, used to a bread-and-water diet and hard knocks. For them, the show here is like Christmas every day. But after a while, they realize that it isn't really Jesus's birthday that often. If they start complaining about how underpaid and overworked they are, someone just says they're five pounds overweight and then they're out on their ear!"

"What about the dressers?"

"They have to behave themselves as well. It's easy to say that they're too clumsy, not fast enough or too talkative. You know, anyone can be a dresser, so . . ."

Virginie, two children, thirty-three years old at the last solstice, was proud of being the oldest employee in the workroom, a dark windowless pit that stank of dyes and sprays. All the same, seniority in a place like this didn't seem to be anything to write home about. But as far as Virginie was concerned, the sewing girls were the most courageous and conscientious group in the entire hierarchy of the Moulin Rouge, and it was they who had triggered off the technicians' strike the previous year.

"Me and Elsa were the ringleaders. That's why they didn't dare fire us. It would have looked too blatant. But twenty-five people did get the sack. They've taken the management to court, but that won't get them into heaven!"

Momo was having problems picturing Michelangelo's little angel on the picket line. He looked with disgust at the old costumes there to be repaired. The smell of sweat and filth filled the tiny room. The fact that Elsa had opted for being near the stage and the show seemed logical enough to him.

"Did she want to become a dresser because she was a masochist?"

"She wanted to dress Manfred because she was crazy about him."

Momo shivered. Once again he glimpsed love and death in each other's arms.

"What about him?"

"We hardly ever heard a peep from him. It was as though everyone else was invisible. But he was a good dancer. Too good for this show. So everyone left him to himself. He was our best lead."

"And do they leave the sewing girls to themselves too?"

"First off, there isn't exactly a queue of people waiting to work in this hole. And then it's hard to criticize your professionalism when you're stitching spangles onto G-strings and sewing on feathers."

In disgust, Virginie went on to explain that what really ought to be criticized was the accumulation of personal waste from the successive groins of the male and female dancers. This show had now been running for ten years, and the panties were beginning to get grubby, especially since all those spangles meant that they couldn't always be laundered.

"Some of the girls get fungal infections on their fingers from handling all this muck. I always wear gloves!"

After an hour's nauseating chat, Maurice now knew everything about how the place operated, the dry-cleaning rota, the washing of tights and ironing of slips. He then headed to a bar to comfort his liver with a double Jack Daniel's. He was unsure how to operate in that operetta atmosphere. Gaping Mouth, the personnel manager, was scared and useless. The show's director, some English woman, had just flown off to Australia. When going out through the hall, he had questioned one of the cloakroom attendants, a former dancer demoted to hats and coats. She complained bitterly about the management. Momo cut her short. He wasn't there to inspect their working conditions! The old dancer calmed down and pulled a long face before observing that the stage director was absolutely rolling in it.

"Very suspicious. There's something definitely not straight about that fat cow!"

Momo nodded in front of the plunging neckline of this ex-queen of the cancan, which was not so straight either, before going out onto the boulevard to call his mother on his mobile. Her quiet calm voice pierced him to the marrow. She wasn't complaining. He'd have preferred her to cry. But no tears were coming. How could he blame her for that? As dry as last Christmas's walnut, he wasn't crying either.

He went back inside the Moulin Rouge, behind the hordes of gaping tourists, then wandered past the bar, through the kitchens and dressing rooms, as far as the theatre, which was now filling up with provincials, Germans and Japanese. Backstage was a confusion of chatter and flutters, and no one seemed at all put out

13

by the fact that two of the young bees in the hive had just been skewered.

Momo remained for some time in the wings, drinking in the show behind the show. The huge python which was slithering over the shoulders of its owner, and which was then rapidly removed by a dancing girl and taken onstage. The enormous horse that unhesitatingly clambered up the tiny spiral staircase, as though lightened and transported by the applause it had just triggered off. The mad rush of powdered and moist naked bodies, which were galloping around, buttocks in G-strings and firm breasts hardly shifting from the motion. The depilated arms reaching out for costumes as they were unhooked. The thirty pounds of spectacular feathered headdresses crushing the backbones of waif-like girls with gleaming stockinged legs. Between two scenes the stage manager explained the hellish pace that had to be kept up if they were going to be able to put on two shows a night.

"Seven days a week. Can you imagine how hard the understudies work? Every day we do link scenes to train up newcomers to replace someone who's ill or pregnant or else blown a gasket and left without warning."

Manfred's understudy was a Swedish giant, standing at nearly seven feet. Between the Viennese waltz and an acrobatic display he performed a striptease right in front of Momo, which enabled him to understand why the Chippendales were so successful. Some men really are beautiful! It was a fact he'd forgotten from spending time in front of his own mirror.

At the end of the second show Maurice had had enough of watching these creatures dashing about and morphing. When he had a drink with a few male dancers at the Rendez-Vous des Artistes, they told him that

14

Manfred had never gone alone with them after the show. He'd had a career as an international dancer in various avant-garde companies, but he never used to talk about that. A little dark-haired man with a pointed nose opined that Manfred was gay, but that they'd never seen him with anyone. A yellow-eyed Bulgarian then declared that he'd once seen him with a handsome American.

"But Manfred wasn't one for confidences. He kept himself to himself."

Momo too. Yet, although he thought of himself as a soul apart, he had so far refused to talk to himself. He went back up Rue Gabrielle at two in the morning, drunk and demoralized. He hadn't come up with the slightest clue. The strike had of course stirred up rivalries and caused some clashes. One of the waiters had told him that, despite the industrial action, the show had to go on, so the rest of the staff had been obliged to replace those technicians who occupied essential posts. This was certainly not social progress, but it could hardly explain why two people had had their throats slit. In any case, Manfred had arrived long after the strike was over. So his opinions at the time could hardly be held against him! What bothered Momo more than anything else was not knowing who exactly the murderer had intended to kill. Him? Her? Both? He hoped that the post-mortem would answer that question. Otherwise, how to find a killer if you don't know who the victim is?

The next day, he woke up painfully to a radio jingle, still absorbed in a dream, that is to say, a nightmare. He'd just pictured his parents in each other's arms, piled up like the corpses in the dressing room at the Moulin Rouge. He stared across the floor from his mattress. Outside, it was raining. A gutter was dribbling down his window. Maurice remembered that he was out of real coffee. He was going to have to make do with another cup of ghastly instant. He pushed back his sheets and blankets with his feet and a lousy mood. Then he stood up on his mattress, dressed in a baggy long-sleeved T-shirt, with a one-humped camel on the front. Momo was freezing his balls off. Spring and rotten weather were synonymous with each other. During his seven-year exile in Normandy, Maurice Laice had attributed those endless spring showers to the rheumatic climate of the Channel coast. How wrong he was! It was just the same in Montmartre, and he hated this time of year more than ever. The heavens emptied their bladder day and night upon an uptight population on the verge of suicide. This season trickled winter into summer, barring one or two sunny periods which brought out the gloomy population in shirt sleeves on to the café terraces to gulp down twenty minutes of sun before a fresh attack from an Icelandic depression.

Maurice stretched with a nauseous yawn. Shrunk with cold, his dick and its playmates dangled beneath the hooves of the one-humped camel. When he put on his slippers, Maurice noticed in horror that his first varicose vein had swollen considerably and turned a Prussian blue. It was sometimes a consolation not having a woman to witness the scene when he got out of bed, especially when the cold and varicose veins took advantage of his bad mood. He slipped on his burgundy dressing gown of Pyrenean wool, went over to the window and tilted downwards the slats of the venetian blind, which merely cast a watery shadow into his damp ground-floor apartment. The shop on Rue Gabrielle where he stayed was a good home in summer. When the weather was bad, however, it was dark and dank. As he only slept and washed there, most of the time he couldn't care less about the complete and utter mess it was in, but some mornings the blues still got to him. When you only have your own arms for comfort, it's hard to keep up hope.

"Stop hurting yourself," he grumbled, kicking his radio alarm, which crackled at him in an attack of feedback. "Give over whipping yourself the moment you get out of bed."

The water was boiling in the old aluminium kettle. Outside, it was now chucking it down. The image of the two corpses, embracing on the pale carpet amid all the spangles and velvet burst back into his mind. He was in a terrible state. On the radio, Francis Cabrel was singing about sleeping with some dame in the Alps, and Momo wouldn't have minded joining him. A bit of R 'n' R with a woman who'd been through the mill already might make him forget that he was in his forties, with neither wife nor mistress, lodging in a pit and living nowhere. An old goat, whose violent stench no longer got the nannies going.

When he left home after three Nescafés, a shower and Bashung's *"Osez Joséphine"*, which accompanied him as he shaved in the bathroom, Momo felt a little better, despite the rain drumming on his cap. He headed straight towards the top of Rue Lepic, via Rue Ravignan and Rue de la Mire.

After his Norman exile, he'd been pleased to get back to Montmartre. There were no two ways about it. This lousy hill was his home, and as soon as he crossed the boulevard into the ninth arrondissement, another world was waiting. Only a Montmartrois could understand that. Further afield, Paris, Normandy, the Loire or Andalusia, it was all the same: not Montmartre!

When he turned down towards 104 Rue Lepic, he

saw his female boss arriving beneath a large orange umbrella. Apparently, she had a clock between her ears. That woman's energy irritated him, but he did have to admit that she loved her job. He'd seen enough of them before, sitting with their butts glued to their office chairs, never lifting a finger. But Commissioner Aline Lefèvre took an active interest. She wanted to know all the details of each case, so as to get an "overview" as she put it, and now she wanted to visit Manfred's apartment.

"Maurice Laice," she announced emphatically. "Are you in one of your moods again this morning? Or is it rheumatism?"

"I've got enough on my plate as it is. I refuse to get rheumatic too."

"If you got laid more often, you'd look less sinister."

"You're young. It's only normal that you've got such a big appetite."

"God forbid that in four years' time I should be as old as you are."

Momo had to admit that at Commissioner Lefèvre's age, in other words, a few dozen months back, he hadn't had her energy. Age isn't everything. Sex is perhaps much more. When not at work, all Aline Lefèvre thought about was getting laid. As a simple believer in "health by orgasm" she practised lovemaking like others take up jogging or tai-chi-chuan, and her tireless evangelizing wore Maurice out.

"You're going to end up going down with something nasty, Maurice Laice. You're in a constant state of high tension. Think of the relief of thunder, lightning and rain. The calm after the storm!"

"I must have Breton or Irish ancestors, I'm more of a one for drizzle and sea breezes."

"That doesn't sound much fun!"

18

They went into number 104. On the sixth floor Manfred's three-room apartment faced south-west, with a view over Paris. You could see, or rather make out through the grimy mist, the tower of Montparnasse, Les Invalides, then the top of the Eiffel Tower, and from one of the western windows, across the gardens that lay behind the buildings, beyond Dalida's house they could vaguely see the shapes of the skyscrapers of La Défense. The apartment had been renovated, with a fireplace in the living room, Jacuzzi in the bathroom and a futuristic fitted kitchen. Such luxury bugged Momo, who was already rummaging through a desk full of papers.

"I thought the dancers in that show were badly paid. We could never rent out a palace like this, could we, Inspector?"

She was teasing. With her lesbian partner, who had a top post in the Ministry of Finance, she shared a four-room apartment let by the city council in Villa Dancourt, just opposite the Théâtre de l'Atelier.

"He owned the place," Momo said, examining some papers. "He bought it two years ago. In other words, before he started working at the Moulin Rouge."

"Any family?"

"His mother lives in Beauvais. She's already been informed, but we haven't heard from her yet."

The doorbell rang. It was the two officers who had been directed to conduct the search. She let them in.

"I'll let you get on with it. Inspector, let's now pay a call on the girl's apartment. I want to take a look there as well. Then you can come back here to follow operations, OK?"

In the street, she looked radiant. Her lipstick shone beneath the sunny light of her umbrella. She was almost pretty despite her large build and square shoulders. And she wasn't butch. Not at all. She was the feminine kind who knows how to walk on high heels and show a bit of leg, and when she laughed she looked like a little girl.

"Do you think she went to see him in his dressing room, and arrived at the wrong moment?"

"I never think; you know that."

At the Corsican angel's place, there wasn't quite the same atmosphere as in Manfred's apartment. It was more Bohemian, a small dark bed-sit with a tiny oil heater, a stand-up shower and an ancient sink. A beautiful brocaded jacket was pinned up on a dummy. On the walls there was a large number of pencil sketches, plus some photos of Manfred.

"How was your evening out at the Moulin Rouge, 'More is Less'?" the blonde commissioner asked from the heights of her suede boots. "Did you find out anything?"

"Apparently Elsa was a bit outspoken. But that's no reason to slice her up along with her lover boy."

Momo stared at the mattress on the floor, which was pushed up along the wall of an alcove. It was so narrow you couldn't even swing a mouse there. Would the Corsican angel have succeeded if she'd had enough time? When she'd become a designer, she'd have told the press about her difficult beginnings in Montmartre. Momo's breast was swelling like a duvet, a plumped-up cushion on which he'd liked to have nestled that dark-eyed angel. How pathetic could you get, falling in love with a stiff? That was him all over. In the end, a corpse doesn't wind you up. All he'd ever know of her was her snowy smile and gazelle-like legs.

"A girl with the hots for a handsome poof, what a tragic photo romance. You'll love it, More is Less. I want to be filled in daily. You know how rapacious I am."

Rapacious was putting it mildly. And yes, Momo was used to it. He knew she needed to be filled in daily! But for the moment, what was getting to him were the photos on the wall: men with muscles, thighs and bollocks. What an era! Where had all the innocent young things gone? Momo thought of his varicose vein and his forty years and three months, in other words more like fifty.

"The girl was a virgin!"

The cop slammed the file down onto the desk, while Maurice cursed into his one-day's stubble. He was fed up with people reading reports before him. It was too much. This station was really going to pot! He relit his cigarillo while pouring himself another shot. Under his ribs, his nerves were knitting large black webs, like one of Piranesi's prisons. How cheerful can you get?

So the beautiful Corsican angel was a virgin! The girl who had haunted his dreams that night had been no more made for pleasure than he was! She hadn't been given the chance to live life to the full. And neither would he, in all probability, because old and knackered as he was, he had still hardly had a taste of honey in his life. You can't be good at everything. But what exactly was he good at?

Once more, he pictured the corpses in that dressing room. Their post-mortem embrace just kept coughing up an image of his parents, their forty-two years of marriage, his father's death, his mother a widow. "Love is stronger than death." His father had framed that sentence, then hung it above the kitchen dresser in their house near Mâcon. It had never occurred to Momo to ask him what it meant. In fact, nothing much ever occurred to him.

He read the forensic report. The weapon used in the double murder was an extremely sharp object, such as an industrial blade. The wounds to the throat had been made brutally and quickly but did not require great physical strength. There had been no struggle. The two victims had been taken by surprise and dazed at the rapidity of the onslaught. The costume rail must have acted as a barrier, stopping the attacker from being sprayed with blood. Momo stubbed out his cigarillo furiously, as though trying to hurt someone. He'd been scared they'd make a mess of his brunette. It all brought back terrible memories, things he didn't really want to go over again. He preferred not to stir up the mud he had in his belly and the slush around his heart. Love. Death. He poured himself another glass of calvados, which warmed his throat and stung his eyes. Then he added a drop of cold coffee and knocked the mixture back in one. His left shoulder hurt. It must be rheumatism, which could only get worse. He could almost smell the retirement home already.

It was impossible to determine the order of the murders formally. From the bloodstains, the pathologist thought that the girl had been killed first, but he couldn't guarantee it, because the bodies had been laid together after the attack. This was just the conclusion Momo had feared. The target had been his little angel. He'd have preferred his pure virgin not to have any shadows cast over her life, just mere bad luck, and to have nothing to do with Corsica and its vendettas. Manfred and his extravagant lifestyle made the whole case look simpler, more tangible, practically kid's stuff!

When he went to L'Oracle at lunchtime, Momo chewed three sticks of cinnamon-flavoured gum simultaneously so as to wear out his mouth and calm his nerves. He needed that. As usual, it was drizzling. As he started along Rue de Panama, he automatically slowed down. Calmed himself. Every time he went to the

Goutte d'Or quarter it felt as if he was in an African market, and the change did him good. He needed to launder his mind, because otherwise he was incapable of changing the music. There was a waltz in his brain. Once one way. Then the next. A pair of corpses, his pair of parents, and him stirring up the shit of memories.

At L'Oracle, Boualem recommended the pork and lentils. Boualem was a cordon bleu, not what you'd expect in such a draughty bistro, with its cooking smells wafting from the kitchens and red wine served in jugs, making lavender stains on the paper table-cloths. He was in his fifties, an Algerian refugee of six or seven years' standing, and the provider of the best advice about wine anywhere in the eighteenth arron-dissement, despite being a practising Muslim and thus never drinking a drop of alcohol himself. He had learned using his eyes, nose and vocabulary. On the blackboard, leaving aside the jugged plonk with nei-ther character nor surprise, the list of the wines of the week was a Tour de France of little vintages. For the past year L'Oracle had been a darling of the trendy guidebooks, such as *Guide du Routard* and *Paris pas cher*, and tourists flocked there, proud of mingling with real Parisians, whom they stared at as if they were the only surviving Indians on the reed rafts of Lake Titicaca.

"I might have found a good buyer for Rémy's stock of books," Boualem said, as he zigzagged between the tables. "I've had a word with Malika."

"Some good news at last! If only he could get his hands on some cash, he could maybe start all over in the provinces somewhere."

Maurice was fretting about Rémy, the only school friend he had left, who was going to have to close down his second-hand bookshop.

"It will be a good thing for Malika. I'm worried about her. She's looking awful."

Boualem liked watching over other people's well-being. Many intellectuals had fled Algeria over the past few years, and Momo imagined that he must have been a magistrate or a university lecturer in Algiers. But he'd never dared ask. He just noticed that Boualem was always in the know about everything. Even about the murders at the Moulin Rouge. He hadn't missed the article in *Le Monde*, which he read daily from cover to cover. *Mysterious and Bloody Double Murder at the Moulin Rouge. Two intertwined bodies have been found in a dressing room. The great Montmartre music hall seems to be dogged by misfortune. Last year, it was badly affected when its technicians went on strike for several weeks.*

"Watch out, Maurice. Intertwining bodies is the work of a sicko!"

This was something Momo preferred not to say to Elsa's mother when she came to the morgue to identify her daughter's body. She was so desperate that he didn't even have the heart to grill her for very long. Well into her fifties, she was thin, with a dry rather angular body, like old Sicilian peasant women in Italo-American movies.

"Yes, I knew she was in love," she gasped. "But I don't know who with."

"I suppose the man she was killed with. There are several photos of him in her apartment."

"She was a serious, hard-working girl. We must get reparation."

Momo bit his unlit cigarillo. What did she mean by "reparation"? A vendetta? Revenge?

"In your family, is anyone linked to any Corsican political movements that are a bit extremist, a bit . . . ?"

He didn't know how to put it. He should have asked

Boualem to give him a crash course on that Corsican hornet's nest. The woman looked at him uncomprehendingly, her head up, in grief, her eyes red.

"I will not allow you to say such a thing, Inspector!"

"What about her father?"

"He vanished off the face of the earth when she was just three, so as far as he's concerned . . ."

Head down, Momo left her after a fairly pointless interview. The weeping mother had just answered his questions with sobs and cries. He grabbed a cab and headed back to Montmartre, to visit a jeweller-cum-sculptor on Rue Burcq. He should know the girl, because she'd been wearing one of his brooches on her red raincoat. When the jeweller saw the piece, he went white, then red and seemed suddenly incapable of drawing a breath.

"I heard about what happened. Isn't it awful?"

He had tears in his eyes. He was a handsome lad of about thirty-five, solid, with huge hands like an old-world blacksmith. The sort who definitely didn't have varicose veins or rheumatism. He sculpted hard matter – stone, marble, wood – into soft items – cloth, blankets, cushions – down to the slightest crease or fold. Some people really do come up with ideas! More modestly, there were small bronzes of women in their daily routines. This sculptor also created spectacular jewellery made of solid silver and lapis lazuli, rock crystals and ebony, which looked more like sacred or ritualistic objects or else precious magic charms rather than supermarket tomfoolery or the trashy gold for the rich on Place Vendôme.

"She posed several times for me . . . I mean, for my bronzes."

He was shifting from red to white. It seemed odd for such a rock to be so emotional.

26

"In a completely honourable way," he added.

Maurice already knew that, thank you very much. The beautiful angel had never gone very far, not with this character or with anyone else. The lad made some coffee in an old espresso machine, which lime-scale had transformed into a steam engine, while explaining that Elsa had come into his workshop one day to ask him about his sculptures and jewellery, and had told him enthusiastically about her first collection of men's wear.

"So I put her in touch with some of the designers around here. They took her very seriously. In fact, I've rarely seen anyone who was so determined. She was really ambitious. It was vital to her. She had such a vision of the future that . . ."

He trailed off. The kid's future had nose-dived so quickly that there was nothing more to be said.

"One of the boutiques on Rue Durantin offered to display her collection this spring. I reckon it would have worked out for her. She had some really original ideas, and in men's fashion there isn't that much competition."

"What about when she posed?"

"Her job at the music hall only just paid the rent. So she needed money to buy her materials and supplies. She told me that dancing girls at the Moulin Rouge earn a bit of pocket money by going out with rich customers. But that was out of the question for her. There was never anything ambiguous about our relationship. She used to tell everyone at the Moulin Rouge about my work. Thanks to her, several girls there have become customers."

All this "nice guy, nice girl" stuff was getting on Momo's nerves. Behind the rock, a photo of his wife and three kids was pinned on the wall. He looked like a happy man. It must be good for the nerves to bang away at stone, then rub it down till it was as smooth as velvet. Above the photo hung a circular copper tray with letters around its rim. Maurice Laice quickly deciphered them: *more is less is more is less is more* . . . He couldn't believe his eyes!

"Did you make that?" he asked.

"No, I bought it in Japan about fifteen years back."

"It's my name," Momo said.

The sculptor didn't get it.

"I'm called Maurice Laice! A psychologist once told me that this phrase can be found on ornaments in the Far East, but I've never actually seen one before."

It had now turned into one of Aline Lefèvre's catchphrases. Had that loony Agnes tipped her off? This was something Momo refrained from asking his boss when he found himself faced with her pearly skin and lacquered lips. She quizzed him. He summarized, explaining that Manfred's mother had shown up to identify the dancer's body before vanishing at once. He hadn't even seen her. So he'd informed the Beauvais brigade that he had to question her as soon as possible.

"They'll keep us posted. For gays, the mother is particularly important, isn't she?"

"Really? That sounds like a sad old cliché to me."

"If you say so."

"There are no two ways about it. You're one of the sort who lifts an elbow more often than a skirt. You can't be trusted."

Momo sighed. He was getting fed up with his boss's one-track mind.

"Does nature still speak for itself when you wake up, Maurice?"

"Sorry?"

"Every morning, nature stiffens male members with a view to procreation, you didn't know that?"

"Well yes, nature does still have its way some mornings."

She was harassing him, and he was losing the plot.

"Anyway, I went to see the estate agents where Manfred bought his apartment. It measured two hundred square feet and was in a very poor condition. He restored the entire place, revamped the walls, replaced the windows, put in a bathroom, the works. It must have cost a fortune. But among his papers, all I found were a few bills for building materials. The work must have been done illegally. What's more, his bank account is extremely quiet. Just the mortgage repayments and the occasional large sum transferred to his mother. As for the rest, he must have been living on cash."

"The usual story apparently."

"I've got their address books. I'll do the rounds."

"Does anyone ever get a smile out of you, Maurice?"

"Don't make me laugh, Commissioner."

"I must take you out one evening. You do realize that there's a life after office hours? And that you can wear other colours apart from brown and black?"

"I'm colour-blind. So brown and black are risk-free . . ."

"And there's no one to take you shopping?"

"It's a bit too late for me to start."

He left his one-track boss, thinking about his only real girlfriend, in the days before varicose veins and rheumatism. A quiet kid who saw colours clearly and found his hands deliciously warm. A brunette with a white face and creamy body, who curled up against him as if he was capable of protecting her. When he really let himself go, he could even remember the smell of the soap they had covered themselves with when they took their first and last shower together before collapsing, asphyxiated by an ancient water heater. Still and silent in a ceramic tomb. Love and death embracing. Like his parents. Like Manfred and Elsa. He'd need another lifetime, perhaps several lifetimes to forgive himself for surviving that disaster. He would need a string of reincarnations to forget that he had been incapable of protecting the only woman who'd ever really trusted him. Maybe that's why he now loved only dead women. What made him even more ashamed was that when he learned at the hospital that his almost fiancée was dead, deep down he'd felt slightly relieved. The death of his future wife had saved him from really taking the plunge into love, that ocean where you never learn to swim. He could stay safe at the bottom of a deep pit, where, twelve years later, he still remained. Hidden. Protected from arrows aimed at his heart. In brown and black. With no one to tell him which colours suited him better.

The squad car was now wailing, stuck in the crush coming out of the Abbesses theatre. Maurice chewed his tongue instead of his cinnamon-flavoured gum. He was finally going off his rocker! Being dragged away from the station that evening just when he was quietly tucking into a ham sandwich and Manfred's address book made his varicose vein throb. When were they going to give him a break? A panicky call from the station on Rue Germain-Pilon about some kind of rave going on in a building that was a regular source of trouble, and now there they were: a bunch of cops, complete with flashing lights and sirens, stuck in traffic at eleven o'clock at night. The theatregoers were looking at them like they were gendarmes in some French movie from the days before Delon and Belmondo had turned into smoked hams. A theatre in the Abbesses quarter! Momo loathed this overly new yet antique monument, splattered here and there with strawberry red, or at least some bright colour or other, which he'd long thought was orange. Those fucking developers had cashed in on his exile in Normandy by getting rid of Le Cochon Rose, Paris's most famous deli, with its doll's house façade and no pretence of looking like a building. Nowadays, the Butte Montmartre was being picked over by a load of culture vultures. Indian dance and modern plays sold better than pig's trotters or snouts in vinaigrette and, at eleven in the evening, here he was, playing cops and robbers amid the

31

thirty-somethings dressed in black and their girls with their painted mouths. Momo wondered how far the transformation of his neighbourhood would go. If it got any more "in", it would implode. Everyone round there was now in the media, was an architect or hack, one of those fucking awful trades that feed off looks like others feed off steak and chips. The cheese shops, tripe shops and butchers were all closing down, to be replaced by ranks of rag shops and hairdressers. What obsession lay behind this mushrooming of barbers and assorted snippers? Maurice found it utterly strange. Ever since school he'd cut his own hair, which was admittedly fine and scant and would obviously get more so, given that time doesn't turn a hair. But it wasn't out of bitterness that he looked down on this multiplication of perm purveyors. Lovers of "the Village" should really be tearing their hair out. No, what was killing Montmartre was its transformation into a shopping mall. Mr and Mrs Cutie came up at weekends from Paris or the suburbs to buy their glad rags in the spanking new boutiques. This carry-on, which would have been unthinkable a few years back, was too rapid, and the contact between fine threads and filthy old long johns was making waves.

The car at last managed to move off. Momo wasn't at all into this raid on Rue "Gerpil". Of all the sculptors who'd given their names to streets in the neighbourhood, Germain Pilon was the one who meant least to him; he was more familiar with Pigalle or Houdon. The building looked a good thirty years old, run down, not a luxury block to start with and getting worse with age. There was no access code or entry-phone. Maurice was flanked by two officers. In front of the letterboxes a lady was wringing her hands, her coat thrown over her shoulders. She was trembling like a birch tree in the wind. She must have been crying her eyes out. They were now Beaujolais Nouveau red. Behind her, looking seven to eight months pregnant, some guy was sucking nervously on a well-endowed Havana.

"Ah, you're here at last, it's appalling, we can't go on like this, the residents are scared, not a week goes by without a fight starting, or someone trying to torch the place!"

"Just about every evening you hear screams, people shoot up in the stairwell day and night, we daren't let our kids come home from school on their own any more."

Maurice decided to cut short the moaners' carry-on. He'd already been to this den of iniquity a year back. Some squatters had been evicted from the ground floor on orders from the prefecture after the official notice had expired. It's as if some places had bad karma. Momo thought how this confirmed every reactionary paranoid copper's adage: shit like this doesn't make roses grow, just bigger shit-heaps. He interrupted the flow to ask what precisely was up this time, and his intervention led the entire party into the garden, because this inn of deniquity actually led out into a garden with, at the end of a path, a charming little two-up-two-down that could have been a prime location. To the left, on the ground floor of the building, stood a large door covered with graffiti.

"It's in there", said the woman with mulled-wine eyes. "We heard terrible screaming."

"No one even knows who the place belongs to, the owner's dead, and his heirs haven't been identified."

After the usual warning, the cops broke down the door. Maurice Laice went in first – "the higher you go, the harder it gets", as Commissioner Lefèvre would have put it. The place stank of piss and rot. Momo played his Maglite over the piles of bins and broken chairs. The floor was scattered with condoms and plastic capsules. It was an old, post-war workshop that used to produce ostrich-feather clothing and accessories. There was still some of the brand's wrapping paper and carrier bags, and some old photos on the walls, including one of Mistinguette in the scantiest of feather garments. Several doors led into smaller workshops. At the back of one of them, a large table was covered with empty tuna cans, ham packets, pots of pâté; the smell of shit got stronger.

Instinctively, Momo bent down to take a look under the table and copped a back view of someone lying on the floor. He slipped in between the wall and table. An oval pool of blood glittered in his torchlight. Set in a frame of Venetian lacquer, a face was pulling a Hieronymus Bosch grimace, with two staring eyes that had given up all hope of ever staring at anything again. Momo gasped for air. An acidic stink of diarrhoea was rising up from the corpse. Without having to touch it, he knew that it was still warm. In the stiff's hand, there was an optic, the sort of thing you dose whisky with, and which others use to smoke crack. Shit! Which was definitely the right word for it. You couldn't get any crazier than a crack smoker, and they all died as crazy as suburban paving. Momo didn't like dealing with this brand of loony. Crack defied all logic, the weather forecast, fans of the horoscope and all other soothsayers. Ever since the roundhouse in the Stalingrad quarter had been cleaned out of pushers of this powder that cleaned whiter than white, cost so little and hooked you on the first hit, dealers had taken to prowling the area between La Chapelle and Barbès, which

34

certainly added to the atmosphere on the Butte. There's more to life than just the theatre!

Momo stepped over the stiff, narrowly avoiding staining his nubuck shoes in the scarlet pool. He hated hot blood, thanks presumably to an atavistic memory from his mother's side: his Burgundian ancestors bleeding a pig, then partying around steaming vats full of scalding intestines and clotted gore. There was no escaping it. He wasn't proud of being half Burgundian three hundred and sixty-five days a year, twenty-four hours a day, and anyone who mentioned black puddings to him got a spray of puke on their shoes. Once the obstacle had been crossed, he regained his balance and his wits. Leaning on the wall, he stared for a while at a spider's web, as big as a crab, whose threads glittered in the beams of his torch. The stench of shit and blood was an insult to his senses. He was on the verge of throwing up when he finally looked down at the corpse and its ghastly wound to the throat. Another slitting? This time it looked like a huge dog bite, from some pit-bull.

Some pit-bull! An hour later Momo was cursing his naivety. Dogs are rarely that mean. The hound that had caused this fatal wound in fact walked on two legs, wore Y-fronts, was probably capable of reading the motorbike pages in *Exchange and Mart*, and of uttering at least a few words not to be found in the latest dictionary of slang. In other words, it was a human being, if someone capable of ripping out his victim's throat with his teeth can be called human. Drugs can perform miracles. The Brits had used cocaine during World War II. And fifty years later its unpleasant by-products were rolling back the borders of savagery and putting the human race back on all fours, teeth bared, ready for the attack, brains relegated to the hindquarters.

"I've never seen anything like it," the medic said. "But I'm pretty certain I'm right. You can still see the marks of teeth belonging to one of our contemporaries."

Momo couldn't even imagine the scene. Man morphed into beast! It was grotesque. Dope and horror movies might make a good match, but actually savaging someone's throat with your bare teeth was still going it a bit. Maurice remembered a girl he'd questioned just after his return to Paris. The cops had picked her up naked and yelling on Place du Delta. During the time she spent at the station, she explained to Maurice how she paid for her stuff by giving blow-jobs. She just adored fucking and smoking crack at the same time. "It's a vicious circle. You can never get enough of it. When you come, it doesn't bring you down to earth. No, it beams you even higher." She'd beamed herself so high that Maurice took her to a refuge for homeless people in the Goutte d'Or for a couple of days. When she got out, she threw herself in front of a bus and was killed instantly.

"I even think that this is a trace of a bridge in the attacker's left premolars," said the pathologist, grimacing behind his magnifying glass. "Can you see that bite there? The one that hasn't torn the skin but just left a mark? It should allow us to reconstruct his dentition, which is as revealing as a fingerprint."

Momo wasn't watching. He was staring at the dirty blade placed on a handkerchief beside the little plastic tubes full of various remains, such as scabs and nails. He thought of his father, whose face must have disappeared by now. But this was no time to be thinking of such horrors. A blade! So this was perhaps the instrument that had killed Elsa and Manfred at the Moulin Rouge. A sharp object. So what? Everyone had blades.

36

School children to sharpen their pencils, and DIY nuts to slice up carpets. These pointless musings were above all an attempt to ignore the noxious stench that was rising from the body. The Moulin Rouge murderer was a maniac. But not some crazed druggie. He'd taken his time to arrange the bodies in a touching scene . . .

"There are burns on the lips. Classic stuff," the pathologist remarked. "A severely infected abscess on the hand. Body covered with cuts. During attacks of paranoia, they often slice themselves up so as to free the creatures they think they have inside them."

So much knowledge was giving this medic one hell of an imagination! As for his identity, there was no need for science. He had his papers on him. Hubert Laboureur, aged thirty-three, living on Rue de Belleville in the nineteenth arrondissement. While the police reinforcements were doing their job decoding traces, picking up clues, scratching at the slightest grain of dust on the corpse, sampling the mud on his heels and taking his footprints, Momo had to go out several times for a breath of fresh air in the garden. He couldn't take any more. All around his varicose vein his calf was beating like an old alarm clock, and needles were digging into his shoulders. Each corpse aged him even more and at this rate he'd be ninety before he officially reached fifty.

Which is just what Aline Lefèvre remarked with her usual discretion. Momo had phoned her on her mobile during a Latino evening at Queen's. One day she'd told him how much she loved the salsa. "I must have lived in the Caribbean in a past existence. I've got Afro-Cuban rhythms in my blood." She thought he looked awful and should take some leave at once. Her mini-skirt revealed her thighs up to the point where they become nameless, and her double magnitude peepers showed that she hadn't gone easy on the pina coladas and caipirinhas.

"Don't push me too far," Maurice blurted out. "Because an evening spent with that stiff under the table is something I'd even exchange for a Christmas party at Club Med. And that's really saying something!"

"More is Less, you've dragged me out of a party, I've had a few too many, and I'm in no mood to put up with your moods!"

She was definitely over the top, pissing him off like this at three in the morning after such a night. He still had the stench of shit in his nostrils, in his stomach and on his shoes. Even the worst sadist would surely have felt some pity for a poor old soul who hadn't even had enough time to finish his ham sandwich. He saw that Aline was thinking things over, which he found rather alarming. She stretched, puffing out her architectural cleavage, which had no need of a puff.

"I was starting to get pissed off with African Paris in that shit-heap of the Goutte d'Or. When the exotic becomes routine, it loses all its charm. I warn you, I'm going to get to the bottom of this!"

A stiff on her patch, and she wanted the whole thing straightened out at once. Orders were orders, and there was no question of disobeying, especially when crack was involved . . . even if it had nothing to do with the first two past the post at Longchamp, drugs were definitely her hobbyhorse. Momo recited his text. This Hubert Laboureur worked in an estate agent's in the nineteenth arrondissement. He'd spent nine months behind bars for drawing up fraudulent leases, then got two months' remission for good behaviour. Behind her alcoholic haze Aline Lefèvre's smile was half crazed, half inane.

"I like your throat victim, Inspector. I agreed to be transferred to the Goutte d'Or because I'd then be given some room to manoeuvre. A difficult neighbourhood for a bit of elbow room in return. And I intend to make the most of it, even if it means stepping outside my field."

Apparently this salsa dancer had no doubts about where her field lay.

"Hand the case over to the Drug Squad. But at the same time we'll follow up the leads ourselves, OK?"

The Latino was out to lunch. Leads? What leads? He already had a double murder on his hands. The thirty-five-hour week was never going to catch on in the force. But La Lefèvre didn't give a damn, absorbed as she was in her basic cop logic.

"Between the Goutte d'Or, Pigalle and Abbesses, there's a paradise for greedy gangsters in silk suits. You know that as well as I do, don't you? The place is going up-market, turning trendy, getting renovated. It's an El Dorado for a certain sort of vermin. You must have learned that at police school, no? It's obviously a distant memory for you, but for me it's still fresh."

A sort of shiver ran through her entire frame. She grimaced for a moment then pulled herself together.

"Take that look off your face, More is Less. Let me give you a . . ."

Her mobile squealed. Maurice wondered if it was some extra cash she was going to give him. Who knows? She was now purring away:

"You're at home now? Both of you? I'm on my way. Open the champagne and try to be good, but not too good!"

Jesus! Who was this creature? A bed full of females and the jugs of a milkmaid.

"I want to know what's going on in that building.

There's something else, apart from the crack. Big money! Speculation! The Drug Squad will do its job, and we'll do ours. I want the big guys who are behind all this. I've obtained permission to take on a young trainee. She's twenty-five, well qualified and born knowing all about the latest information technology. You'll see: she'll dazzle you."

Momo yawned. Big guys, information technology and qualifications . . . What a carry-on.

"Don't look so enthusiastic, More is Less! I'm giving you tomorrow morning off. I don't want to see you before two or three in the afternoon."

He reckoned that she wouldn't be in for work that early either, she'd be sleeping off her threesome, which she'd kicked off rather late. He had almost wished her a good fuck but thought better of it. He wasn't that much of a miserable bastard.

Don't move. The clotted blood is soaking into her blue cotton scarf. It's so cold. Her mouth has been closed by the coagulated red. Don't scream. Concentrate on the regular beating in your chest. One heart for two bodies. Occasionally, the killers hurl fistfuls of words over the pile of bodies. They search them, strip them, shift them about. Don't move. Barely breathe so as not to give away this forgotten life.

At five in the morning Momo slumped down like an oldster in a home after his soup, pills and herbal infusion. He woke up in his mother's arms. His father's skeleton was dancing the tango to a Guy Marchand number. Maurice would have preferred Carlos Gardel, but nightmares don't always have the good taste you might expect of them. From his mattress on the floor, he opened a puffy eye on an off-white pair of Y-fronts, the first item of the mess piled up on the ancient floor tiles in his hovel. It wasn't even seven-thirty and pneumatic drills were already making the walls shake. The windows were rattling like fairy bells. More building work. It never stopped. Paris was just one big construction site, four hundred and fifty days a year. For once he'd been given the chance to have a lie-in, and now he was being shaken awake by an earthquake! It was more than he could take.

So he drank his Nescafé sitting in his woolly slippers with his camel. It looked as if the crack under the *Pierrot le Fou* poster had got wider. He could almost slip his little finger into it. What a great start to the day! It was almost a shame he wasn't in agony from appendicitis or acute pneumonia so they could rush him off to hospital, where he could wrap up his old bones for a few days so as to avoid the surrounding crap. Meanwhile, he had some time off. A feeling for leisure should be taught at school instead of multiplication tables. What the hell was he going to do with himself?

Outside, the renovation of the gas pipes covered a good three hundred yards of Rue Gabrielle. It would take weeks, or so it said on the sign that apologetically pleaded for "your comfort and safety". It wasn't raining, which was already something, but a damp wind was flowing from the languid grimy sky. There was no danger of catching a case of early spring sunstroke. Maurice sought solace at Le Dymey with a shot of calvados. His mother was on his mind. He had to go and see her. She was planning on putting the family home up for sale. Momo suddenly realized how losing your roots sometimes meant losing your marbles. It must be too hard for her to bear a family house that had become the terribly precise black box of an ex-person's movements and gestures. In love stories as in earthquakes, it's the length of time they last that causes most damage. He pictured his parents kissing thirty years before in the brand-new fitted kitchen of the modest house that was to be for holidays and then retirement. Now that simple residence had become a funeral monument to grief and sorrow. The survivor must be lost in that place of defeat. And her son was incapable of suggesting any means of escape.

He left Le Dymey and went up towards Rue Burcq, stopping in front of the sculptor's shop. One of the small bronzes in the window depicted a couple embracing. It seemed that, day and night, Momo was being pursued by intertwining couples, living or dead. He went inside. The goldsmith-cum-sculptor shrank back from him. Another nice thing about being a cop was seeing the joy you spread whenever you show up somewhere. A hoard of bad memories of school, bad marks, military service, jail, sadistic parents, slaps and beatings welcome you everywhere.

"How much is the couple in the window?"

The sculptor recovered his smile and placed the bronze on the counter. Momo asked some unofficial questions, while examining the boxwood tools used for hammering and beating silver. He spent two hours with the artist, who agreed to sell him the bronze on a one-year loan and at a discount of fifteen per cent.

"In homage to the kid."

"I didn't know her at all. And I'm pretty sure I wouldn't have appealed to her much: an old cop as sad as Sunday."

"She was really something! She didn't talk much, but I'm sure she'd suffered. Life hadn't been a bed of roses for her. Even though she was young, she gave the impression of having been through a lot."

Momo pulled a face, removed a stick of cinnamon-flavoured gum from its foil wrapper and folded it into his mouth. He didn't want to know. For him, the brunette in the red raincoat was a pure and innocent angel: you can believe in any old crap sometimes, it takes your mind off things. In fact, he hadn't even contacted the police in Bastia. Maybe he could ask the new assistant who had just been taken on to deal with that, because as far as he was concerned Corsica was out!

It was almost noon when he walked down Rue Aristide-Bruant, his loving couple hooked under his arm, to Rémy's shop on the corner of Rue Véron. The sign had been the same for the past thirty years. The old-fashioned letters, painted white with black edging, read SECOND-HAND BOOKS: BOUGHT AND SOLD. The worm-eaten wood was covered with flaky black paint dotted with blue, white and red graffiti, strange ideograms in tricolour tones. Maybe it was because of these medieval premises that Momo had decided to set up home in a shop on coming back from Normandy. During his childhood, he had dreamed of living like his friend Rémy, on the ground floor with a large window looking out onto the street. To play at living in a shop. And not in a box like the other kids. How lucky Rémy was! He also shared the lives of thousands of people in books. He fed on their adventures, was full of their mysteries, was a bigger, handsomer hero than the other boys of his age. His father had read everything, and so experienced practically everything. His mother, who was a painter, invented dream universes and creatures. Meanwhile Momo was suffocating between the bulky furnishings in his parents' two-room apartment on Rue Coustou. He lived with his eyes closed, starched into the thickness of reality, the hell of routine, with a father who worked for Renault and a mother who was a fishmonger on Rue Lepic. Do those who dream with their eyes open realize how lucky they are?

Momo went inside. The same ring of the bell as from thirty, twenty, ten years ago. The same dusty smell of ink and old paper. The same dense silence guarded by the books. Just like thirty years back, the left-hand wall was reserved for Montmartre: Carco, Bruant, Mac Orlan, Dorgèles. While their mates were lapping up Marcuse, Sartre, Jung and Kerouac, Rémy and Momo savoured those adventurers of old Montmartre, those explorers of moods and sorrows, lovers of ordinary people and places of disrepute. Momo gently stroked a few dog-eared dust jackets, letting himself drift into an old man's nostalgia. In the stockroom Malika didn't look up. She was at her bench working on her bindings. She was in another world of stiff cardboard, decorated paper, glue and leather. She was pressing, easing and cutting, her face lit by the care she applied to her work. She looked even younger than her twenty-five years as she laboured to preserve and embellish. Momo walked on towards the smell of glue and kidskin. In the old days there hadn't been a book-binding workshop in the store. Rémy had set one up in the stockroom when Malika had moved in with him two years ago. She got up, kissed him shyly, then started slipping thread into her pale wooden sewing press. As absorbed as she was, Momo didn't dare look at her. Malika was too beautiful, too luminous for him. She started to unstitch a book, carefully removing the gatherings from the back of the cover. Momo thought how he would never have the patience to remain there for hours, leaning over his hands. He grabbed one of the books from a small shelf. Quarter-bound, with brown leather on the back and green marbled paper on the boards, it was smooth and soft in his hands thanks to its new coat, which made him forget the yellow pages, dotted with red. It was Carco's *Jésus-la-Caille*.

"It was a cult book, for Rémy and . . ."

"Especially for you," said Rémy as he entered.

Pale, with a haggard face, he went over to Maurice and took him in his arms. The affection of his only real friend did Momo some good. He gave him a hug and felt better at once. And yet Rémy was in a real mess. His shop was soon going to close. The lease was almost up and the owner was claiming a rent increase that he would never be able to pay. It was certain that this medieval store looked out of place in a now trendy neighbourhood, and the hairdressing salon next door was dying to expand. When were the Indians going to come along and scalp those fucking cowboys with their scissors and combs?

Rémy's hand was affectionately placed on the nape of his schoolmate's neck. Its soothing presence finally removed Momo from the freezer where he'd been since his father's funeral. So, snuggled up together like a pair of kids, they abandoned Malika and went back into the shop.

"How's your mother?"

"She seems to be doing OK. I'll have to go and see her soon."

For Rémy it must have been even harder, ten years back, when he'd lost both his mother and his father in a car accident. They too had remained entwined together to the very end. Momo was now thoroughly sick of this rerunning image . He decided to stick to things concrete.

"Boualem has maybe found a buyer for your stock. Did Malika tell you?"

Rémy glanced round in panic at his wife, like a drowning man who's not even trying to swim. He thought of her as a child, without the slightest independence, incapable of looking after herself. Momo envied his capacity for devotion. He would so have loved to dote on someone, to tremble with delight.

"Uh, no, she didn't tell me anything. I'll go and see Boualem at L'Oracle . . ."

Burning with anxiety, Rémy looked old, broken and done-for, and it really got to Maurice.

"A little Jack Daniel's?"

"Just a little one, then."

Rémy poured a triple measure for each of them. Momo leaned on a sideboard covered with illustrated books from the turn of the twentieth century. He knew that Rémy hated not being able to provide anything better for Malika than the dark poky apartment on the first floor, at the top of the spiral staircase. Living here was no longer a dream nor even Bohemian, it was quite simply shit.

"Will you stay for lunch?"

48

"No. I'm only here because of Manfred Godalier. You were in his address book."

"I saw he'd been murdered in the papers," Rémy murmured.

He stared at the wall of books as though submerged by the weight of destiny. Then he muttered:

"He used to go to the dancing class on Rue Coustou. That's why I knew him."

Momo grimaced. Rémy must have seen Manfred as the young energetic dancer that he'd once been. As a teenager, Rémy had been the best-looking lad in Lycée Jacques-Decour, stopping the periods of all the girls just by looking at them. The first to play the guitar, to dance rock 'n' roll, to have a bed-sit, to get laid. He was frightened of nothing. He played around with booze and drugs, with never a hangover or a bad trip. As a cultivated, heroin-taking, cocaine-sniffing ladies' man about town he dazzled his contemporaries with quotes from Rimbaud and Mac Orlan. As an adult, he became a stunning dancer, flitting between companies in New York and Moscow, Prague and London. And then came his parents' accident. Three months later a surgeon messed up an operation on a malformation of his spinal chord. Six months in hospital. Impossible to start dancing again. Another operation a year later. Another foul-up. This succession of disasters made him abandon his body as others lay down their guns. His back dogged by collapse, his right leg constantly burning with sciatica, he had taken over his father's second-hand bookshop. But nourishing others with poems and stories had never really replaced dancing. He had started drinking. No doubt to forget his other self, the one he could no longer hope to keep up with.

"We had a drink together once or twice," Rémy went on.

"I've been told he didn't drink."

"He was more into Perrier with ice and a slice, so far as I can remember. It was one of his problems."

Momo wondered how Rémy could still give lessons twice a week, twisted up as he was. Bringing back to life the ritual movements of the arabesque, *détiré* and *sissone* must be pretty disillusioning. His dancing days were over. His muscles, which had once been harmoniously distributed thanks to exercise, had shifted and gone limp. His neck sank into his shoulders, his waist was plump and his body bent.

"I think he lived in the States for some time," he murmured.

"Three years in New York."

Momo looked at his mate's wrecked and aged face. He was as gutted as a fish and now lived only by proxy: others did the dancing for him. He had married a young Algerian girl so that she could get French nationality, and for a time his gargoyle's face had recovered its grace. But adversity had caught up with him. It was as if it had decided to dog him till the end.

"Cheers!" said Rémy, pouring out a third ration of Jack Daniel's.

He stared at Maurice.

"I'm not on your list of suspects, I hope?"

Maurice's guts tightened. It was all too much for Rémy. Sorrow, grief, renouncement, the building of impregnable walls, the projecting of cold, black figures on each moment of time, which only the warm fumes of alcohol made bearable.

"He never mentioned anything special?"

"In New York he used to work for a company run by some Dutch woman . . ."

"Elke Patrice. Yeah, I know."

"We had a few mutual friends, people I used to dance with who have become choreographers."

"But it's odd you were in his address book, no?"

Momo sensed Rémy's annoyance. Having an old friend come round sniffing like a bloodhound was more than he could take. Maurice sighed. He wasn't going to let this masochist's job get between him and his only mate. The only person he'd spent every day with from the age of eleven to eighteen, at a time when years lasted eons and were full, not yet reduced to dust.

Momo gazed at the backs of the books lined up on the shelves. He was by the letter "R": Rilke, Rimbaud, Rezvani. Malika was still at her bench. She wasn't looking at them or listening to them. She remained in another world, with her leather bindings. She was now permanently absent, ever since they'd found Alya, their two-month-old baby, lying dead in her crib. Cot death is an injustice, a punishment: indisputable proof of God's incompetence. Malika never mentioned it. In fact, she spoke less and less. The passionate love Rémy had for her apparently made no difference. Being someone's reason to go on is perhaps less of a compensation and more like a prison.

Momo apologized: "I just thought it'd be less unpleasant to talk informally at your place, rather than down at the station . . ."

"Of course."

"OK, so you've got nothing to say; I won't keep you till Christmas!"

He offered him his box of cigarillos. The former dancer took one. Momo raised his lighter between them, and its bluish flame created a fleeting moment of calm, almost of peace.

"I'll type out a short report then bring it round for you to sign. There's no reason for you to come in."

Rémy nodded, then offered another round.

"No thanks, I think I've had enough," Momo said.

He walked along the wall, going down the alphabet as far as the letter "C", where he pulled out *Requiem of the Innocents* by Calaferte, whose *The Way it Works with Women* he had really enjoyed.

"I want this rebound in blue leather."

"You'll have to see about that with Malika. Sure you won't stay for lunch?" Rémy asked.

"No thanks!"

Momo picked up the packet he had purchased from the sculptor and unpacked the bronze. Rémy commented:

"That's by the bloke on Rue Burcq, isn't it? I really like what he does."

"It's for you," said Momo. "You deserve it, both of you . . . I . . ."

Rémy took hold of the sculpture. Momo saw a glimmer of past happiness pass over his face. He turned towards his wife and said, like a child:

"Look how lovely it is, my darling! It's for us!"

Malika looked up towards the entwined couple. Tears were pouring from her staring eyes. Rémy took her in his arms:

"My darling, my little darling . . ."

Momo looked at his feet. He felt terrible. Once again, he'd put his foot in it. All the same, he just couldn't see why Rémy treated his wife like a babe in arms. Malika pecked Maurice's cheek.

"You've got no choice now, you're going have to stay," Rémy decided.

When Maurice got to the station, a young lady was sitting behind his desk. What a cheek! She was petite, like Minnie Mouse, with a pointed snout. She was grinning with elated enthusiasm, which got straight on Momo's nerves. He hated people who were always smiling, with their brains tingling with delight, always looking out for life's little silver linings, no matter where they found them! Momo imagined that they must have a clothes peg at the back of their necks pulling their lips up to their ears. Such cheery types depressed him completely.

"Let me introduce you to Caty," the boss said, coming in behind him. "This is Inspector Maurice Laice, or 'More is Less'. Although 'Less is More' would suit him better. He's more competent that he looks."

"In that case, he must be really extremely competent," Caty giggled, her lips up to her lobes.

Momo gritted his teeth:

"You've got some cheek talking about looks. I suppose I'm going to be called a misogynist, but when you get bitten even before you put your hand out, it's enough to turn you rabid!"

"Don't worry, Caty. He isn't as grumpy as he sounds. Just a little in need of affection. I'm banking on you to give him back his sunny disposition."

Momo felt the stink of mustard bite into his nose. Why didn't he tell the silly bitch that he didn't even want this mousy thing to shine his boots? It was a shame he was so nice and polite! He stood there, dumbly waiting for it to all be over. Apparently, when you're angry, you shouldn't say anything or do anything before reciting the alphabet first, preferably in Japanese, which is safer, but Momo was no linguist.

"Pleased to meet you, Inspector," the mouse said, its mouth stretched horribly.

"Caty will work mostly in the office. I know how paperwork gives you a migraine. But she's happy to spend weeks between the computer, the phone and the Web."

"We should get along fine then," Momo murmured.

"She's already been through our handsome dancer's bank accounts. Apparently you missed rather a lot of things."

Momo took the blow unflinchingly.

"He had a second account in a private bank. A large part of his income came from a certain Philip Leigh, an American living in New York."

Maurice was furious about the gaps in his work being shown up like this. But he was probably wrong to be. They were giving him an office-loving secretary. It was incredible! Aline Lefèvre purred on:

"As for our victim on Rue Gerpil, apart from working in an estate agent's in the nineteenth, he also organized raves. And we found two rather nasty vials in his trouser pockets. GHB. That was not part of your generation's pharmacy, but . . ."

"Despite being utterly useless, I do read the papers," Maurice butted in. "So I happen to know that GHB is a synthetic drug, originally developed as an anaesthetic."

"Not bad! Do you know about this stuff, Caty?"

"Not at all."

"Bodybuilders liked to use GHB twenty years back to

help develop their muscles. Then some druggies discovered its incredible effects. It increases your sensuality and causes short-term amnesia. In the USA it's called the 'date rape' drug, or the 'easy lay' or 'the sex express'. GHB is odourless and tasteless, so when slipped in a girl's drink, the guys can then rape her and next day she won't remember a thing."

She was as taut as an elastic band about to break. Her eyes were sparkling. Momo watched her trembling lips and hands. What wild mood swings she had!

"A dream drug for men, don't you think?" she said, staring murderously at him.

He felt like slapping her. Really, this was more than he could put up with. Why couldn't she aim her anti-male attitude at someone else?

"You know perfectly well that I'm not a real man, Commissioner. Nobody's perfect."

"When taken in large doses with alcohol, GHB can cause respiratory depression leading to a coma. So, Inspector, it was just like I was saying the other day. This trendy neighbourhood is thirsty for novelty. And I don't think I was so very wrong about that!"

Momo realized that synthetic drugs must be one of her hobby horses. She had some score to settle with them: that much was sure.

"And who does that old feather factory belong to?" he asked, to change the subject.

"It's a joint ownership. It used to belong to a company called Plumier. The CEO died ten years ago on some island in the Caribbean. Caty's looking into it."

Aline Lefèvre slipped a hand under Momo's arm and guided him out into the corridor.

"If you continue to go around with your chin on the ground, I'll hang a sign round your neck marked BEWARE OF THE DOG."

"I only bite people I've known well for a very long time."

She led him into her office.

"Welcome to my kennel!"

The walls were covered with photos of the world's most beautiful women: Bardot, Gardner, Cardinale and Grace Jones accompanied Aline Lefèvre's darling from the Ministry of Finance, a sort of red-headed version of Catherine Deneuve.

"Caty's going to draw up a detailed report about the history of who owns what in that building on Rue Gerpil, then check out everything that's been going on round there in terms of town-planning, property developers and investors. I've got a source in the Drug Squad who will keep us informed of everything that's going on in terms of crack and synthetic drugs. I want to find out what fiddles involve people who go around ripping out throats with their bare teeth. As for the Moulin Rouge, we're going to have to chase up this American benefactor."

"I've been going through Manfred's address book. I've been paying my visits and I'll give you a full report. I also went to the dance class on Rue Coustou and spoke to the teachers and students. He doesn't seem to have been close to anyone."

"What about his mother?"

"Still out of the picture. The boys in Beauvais are looking out for her. Meanwhile, the supposedly stinking rich director is still in the outback, two hundred miles from Sydney."

"Speaking of walkabouts, I've booked you a ticket for Bastia. Because if we wait for the Corsicans to give us a report on the girl, you'll probably be retired with your feet up by the time we get it."

"I'm not as old as I look, you know."

"Unfortunately for you, the lack of a sense of humour accelerates the aging process."

"So do Corsican sun rays."

"For Christ's sake, More is Less, you really have a gift for taking everything the wrong way! Do you also suffer from a fear of flying?"

"I was imagining the hearty greetings at Bastia airport. It's a well-known fact that the Corsicans just love people coming along to nose around in their affairs."

"But mother's here, my little one! She won't let you down. My ex will take care of you."

Momo absent-mindedly gazed round at the eyes in the photos. Her ex? What ex? The red-headed Deneuve was in the present, so who was her predecessor?

"In a previous lifetime I used to be married. No one's perfect."

"To a Corsican?"

"A Breton. It was in the days when I still thought I could love beasts with five legs."

"A fifth leg? You're idealizing our modest members a bit!"

"How right you are! I have problems with the single-track minds of people with a variable member. At the beginning, like all women, I was fascinated by the instrument, by its sensitivity, its hydraulics, its ability to malfunction, its adaptability. But then, like many of my sisters, I realized that we lost out all along the line. The owner of the instrument is always more in love with it than with his partner. In the end, you give in. Three is a crowd! Why do men compete with their women in their own Y-fronts, can you explain that, Inspector?"

"You know me, if I didn't have to go and piss occasionally, I wouldn't even remember I owned one of your so-called marvellous instruments . . ."

"Not even in the morning? I thought you told me . . ."

"Generally, the mood I'm in when I wake up puts even nature to flight. So, anyway, your Breton is now in Corsica?"

"Commissioner Lefèvre, which will not be much of a change for you. He allowed me to keep his name. In fact, we're not even divorced. He'll pull as many strings for you as you want."

But all Momo wanted there and then was to be left alone. At the end of the afternoon, he left the station feeling completely done in. The smiling mouse with the automatic clothes-peg grin had broiled his brains with the Internet and its networks of police records, solicitors' files and land registries in order to explain to him the comings and goings on the property-owning slopes that led down from Abbesses to Pigalle. Momo felt like he'd been put on a job opportunities scheme, a barely disguised incitement to suicide. It was all too squeaky-clean for him. It stank of Vichy, order, lists.

He went straight to L'Oracle to get a breath of African air and stuff down a prune and almond tagine. He felt as though he'd been reincarnated as an Arabian prince, whose harem were busying themselves languorously around him. Some women were doing a belly dance while others massaged his back and feet as he ate. The diced lamb, scented with cumin, cardamom and nutmeg, melted in his mouth. Such pleasures made Maurice forget his state of irritation. Summer was coming up at last. Between his temples, one and a half bottles of Sidi Brahim red were blowing a mid-July heatwave through the Valley of Death, thus evaporating all his glooms.

Boualem religiously explained his ideas about tagines. The fine strips of crystallized lemon gave an almost acidic bitterness to the caramelized sauce, toned down by the sweetness of the onions, while also being heightened by the spiciness of the ginger. He recited his recipes as though murmuring a prayer, as good a way as any to escape from the shit of life. It was in prison that he had learned hundreds of recipes by heart. "To keep my taste for life!" And the technique had proved effective. When he spoke about cooking, his listeners started to dream along with him. On the strips of courgette, sliced with a potato peeler, then blanched for two minutes, were placed filets of red mullet, which had been fried for forty-five seconds on the skin side, and thirty on the flesh side. A warm mixture of black olives, pine nuts and various sorts of pepper was then sprinkled across that movingly green and pink landscape. Shredding, adding water, binding, diluting, slicing and thickening sauces were, for this poet, a pleasure that exceeded any erotic endeavour. His culinary litanies wiped out from his memory the massacres which made up the daily life of his country and which he never mentioned. This Algerian must have had big problems on the other side of the Mediterranean.

"I imagined you must have been a university professor in Algiers. But in fact you were a cook, is that right?"

"You could call it a certain form of cooking but not always easy to digest," Boualem replied before shooting off to another table.

Efficient and precise, Boualem swerved between his tables like a toreador. He dashed from the far side of the room with a clean fork because a customer had dropped his on the floor. Even with his back turned he could tell the difference between a falling knife, fork or spoon and know from which table and which place it had fallen. A consummate artist!

Momo never knew how he got back to Rue Gabrielle. He had a blackout, or, more exactly, a black hole. He couldn't remember dragging himself into his bed. Above the vibrations of the pneumatic drills, it seemed to him that someone had been knocking on the shop window for some time, because the noise had been part of his dreams over the last few nightmares. In the half-light the red figures on the radio alarm said it was eight-fifty. Sleeping with no memory of sleep is even more tiring than staying up all night. Momo bent his knees, managed to reach a fairly stable vertical position, threw a Pyrenean woolly over the camel's back while wondering if he'd actually undressed himself the night before and put on his T-shirt. He went to the door, guided by the terrible stench that was issuing from his mouth. Early-morning tagine and Sidi Brahim would make an effective insecticide.

"Did I wake you up? I'm so sorry. If I'd known, I'd . . ."

This woman looked pretty huge to him, a little taller than he was. Old and ugly. Between forty-five and fifty, with a thin slightly wrinkled face, no make-up, with large almost rectangular eyes . . .

"What do you want?"

"I'm the mother," she said.

Momo stared at her as she swayed. Then he vaguely realized that he was the one who was swaying and she was standing straight in front of him. He furrowed his brows even though he knew that it didn't make him look any the brighter. The mother. Why ever not? He thought of primitive earthenware sculptures of women with massive hips. Mothers of humanity. But this one was no piece of pottery, more like a scarecrow, but with sparkling eyes. They made your skin tingle when you looked at them, even though she was utterly unscrewable.

"Manfred's mother," she added.

Momo noticed with approval that her smile altered her eyes but hardly affected her mouth. That was a piece of good news. At that moment, despite the fog hanging in his brain, he recognized the ageless, sexless person in the Polaroid that he had found in the Moulin Rouge dressing room after the murder. Manfred's mother! She looked more like a transvestite from Michou's or Madame Arthur's.

"Come in," he muttered, slipping behind the door.

That was when he drank in the true horror of the situation. He caught a close-up of his varicose vein on his left calf, and his Pyrenean pullover hanging down over his lifeless cock and balls. Then, further up, above an Adam's apple no one had wanted to nibble for ages, between the two strips of grey beard, the smell of half-digested tagine between his teeth. What a wreck! He heard the old woman gingerly clear her throat and say:

"I'll make some coffee if you like. I've brought croissants."

The red figures on the radio alarm informed Momo that Manfred's mother had now been there for an hour, and he hadn't noticed the time go by. Despite the gallon of coffee that he had got through, he felt terrible, with his morning hangover, hyena breath and dishevelled hair. He must be looking even older than her. It wasn't with the young and beautiful Elsa that he should compare this woman, but with himself, green around the gills, slack-bellied and with calves destined for varicose veins.

He poured out some more coffee. He would have liked her to stay, her presence did him good. He liked her smile, which didn't wipe out the sadness of her face but which did light up her eyes to the full. This woman was relaxing. She almost made him want to find his courage again. She would not demolish him or make a fool of him. It gave him some hope for the humanity of the human race. Perhaps age and phys-ique had condemned the dancer's mother to a quiet life. Although she did become slightly less hideous when she spoke. Her hands and wrists sketched out graceful patterns in the air. Was it because of her job? She was a glassblower. Like Elsa, like Manfred, she was a creator. The admiration Maurice had for artists had long ago relegated him to the ranks of the sad and impotent. He remembered in wonder a glassblowing workshop he had visited with his parents when they were camping in the Auvergne. A volcanic heat, the light of a conflagration and, at the end of the blower's rod, the bubble of glass taking shape. With his mouth agape, he had watched the men remove the glass from the oven, then tame and stretch it. This play with fire and air seemed to him to be sacred, and a dull sadness drifted over him. He was eight, but he already sensed that his hands would produce nothing that was beautiful, and that his mind would forever remain in that dense sluggishness that is typical of perpetual spectators.

"My son was killed by accident, it was a mistake, he was in the wrong place at the wrong time."

Her voice was muted, slightly throaty, and Momo felt rocked. He had no need to ask any questions, because she was telling him everything about Manfred, without holding back, as though he was still alive. And yet she was no mad woman, just a touch eccentric. Given that he was dullness made flesh, the pair of them made a good balance.

"Could he have witnessed something he shouldn't have seen in the more or less distant past?"

"I'd have known about it."

She spoke in a soft voice, without getting worked up, without even pressing her point, with the firmness of certitude.

"He told you everything?"

"I don't think I'm a possessive mother, if that's what you mean. Manfred took more care of me than I did of him. His father and I divorced when he was eight. And he wanted custody. I agreed. In Amiens, where his father taught at the university, Manfred's life was easier, more social. In Picardy, the winters are long, and in my workshop the heating isn't very good. I always saw Manfred regularly. His father gave him a wonderful education, with music and dance. He's an emeritus professor of biology."

She then launched into such warm praise of the father that Momo even started to wonder why they'd divorced. The ex-husband had now been living in New Caledonia for six years.

"Manfred worked for extremely prestigious contemporary dance companies. He came back to France when I fell ill. He managed to get a few contracts. Then he decided to take a job in the show because it was near where he lived, while he was also converting his apartment. It was handy. And then, he found the experience amusing."

"What about his love life?"

Manfred had been in love with an American man he'd met in New York. Maurice felt a fleeting sensation of gratitude to the new trainee, who had provided the information. He could now follow the story more easily.

"Philip Leigh?"

"That's right. Manfred experienced true love with him. And that's important. When you have really loved, death is less awful."

Maurice's heart contracted. Once again, he pictured that sentence that his father had hung over the dresser in that house near Mâcon: "Love is stronger than death." It was the second time that this glassblower had mentioned love as an antidote to death. How on earth could she think such things? Did she really believe it?

He made some more coffee. Sitting on the arm of a chair, she had taken off her raincoat. She was wearing jeans and a black sweater. He saw how she was sitting bolt upright and stood up straighter, adjusting his dressing gown. She must be feeling sorry for him. He lit a cigarillo and tried to pick up the thread of his questions.

"And this American helped him, I suppose?"

The novel thought occurred to him that he was far more used to being confronted by people who call for help and who no one answers.

"Manfred owned the apartment on Rue Lepic. But it was also Philip Leigh's Paris lodgings. Philip paid for the purchase and the renovation work. It was small change as far as he was concerned. Money doesn't count for the heir of one of the largest shareholders in an international pharmaceutical company. He has more spending-money every month than you or I could earn in several years."

"I hope you earn more than I do," Momo observed.

"I'm afraid you'd regret it if we exchanged bank accounts, Inspector. All the same, Manfred worked a lot. He was a model for a brand of ready-to-wear clothes. But that was still not enough for him to help me."

"Your son maintained you?"

"Lymph cancer stopped me from working for two years. Manfred paid for my treatment, convalescence, physiotherapy, rest homes, everything, down to the last centime. Philip gave Manfred a valuable painting so that he could sell it to pay for everything. It probably saved my life. Manfred's father was never informed."

"Why not? If he's such a wonderful guy?"

"He's started a new life on the far side of the world. He's got two other children. I wanted to spare him."

For a moment, Momo wished that he had experienced such things, but nothing important had ever happened to him. Even Manfred, despite his youth, had savoured more of life than he had. His mother was finding some comfort for her grief in the fact that her son really had lived. Dancing, love, a mother to protect. But Momo didn't even take care of his own mother. He behaved like a swine! He lit another cigarillo. Animals hate tobacco, which at least proved he was partly human.

"Why didn't this Philip contact us after Manfred died?"

"He doesn't know. He and Manfred haven't seen each other for six months. It was a separation of convenience. Philip is going to get married next summer . . ."

"So it's more the wedding that's 'of convenience', isn't it?"

"Of course. But Manfred understood that and accepted it. They were intending to meet up again on a regular basis in Paris and New York later on. Meanwhile, they had vowed not to contact each other. Philip calls me from time to time from Los Angeles to get news. When they were living together in New York, they used to come over for a few weeks in the summer to my workshop in Picardy. I taught Philip how to blow glass. It was one of his greatest pleasures in life."

"And you haven't called him?"

"He always calls me. I suppose the next time will be after his honeymoon."

Momo poured out more coffee. This woman was gradually dispelling all of the mysteries surrounding the dancer and his beautiful apartment and loads of cash. So was the real victim the Corsican angel? He really didn't like the idea. He wanted that girl to rest in peace, and he had not the slightest desire to rummage through her ashes.

He stood up and stretched. He had trouble getting his thoughts together. In any case, the glassblower's tale was unconvincing. It was all about the great and the good, and it didn't fit with her looks, with her curly red hair around her unmade-up face; it didn't fit with her ill-heated workshop, with his shop-cum-apartment, its dampness and chaos. Behind a corpse, there's always filth waiting to be turned up, as though human beings are only there to conceal all the shit that finally bursts out when their hearts stop beating. He added a drop of calvados to his coffee to chase away the picture of Elsa and the dancer in each other's arms, dowsed in blood.

"Did he ever mention the little sewing girl who was killed with him?"

"No. Lots of women were after him. He was magnificent, tall and dark, with burning eyes he inherited from his father, who's originally from Pakistan."

Momo almost asked her how it was that, from her icy studio in Picardy, she got to hang around with New Caledonian Pakistanis and Americans from the Big Apple and California. When listening to her, it sounded as though the planet was a village, and that panicked him. He felt as if he was crossing an ocean every time he went over the road into the ninth arrondissement. This woman was definitely not made of the same stuff as he was.

Talking about crossing seas, he shouldn't forget that he was off to Bastia, and his plane was leaving at three in the afternoon from Orly. He at least had to take a shower, then drop in to tell the mouse what the glassblower had blown in his ear.

"Whatever happened, Manfred never had any affairs with women. He was faithful to Philip. Since their separation, he'd been practising abstinence. I know that. We often talked about it. I thought he was wrong."

"Why?"

"Let's just say that it isn't my conception of love."

Momo couldn't repress a shudder. She'd already said "it isn't my conception of death" when talking about grief. It seemed to him that she was talking too much, trying to convince him that her son was perfection made flesh. But he was paid, albeit badly, to know that such things were never true.

"Feelings and principles make a bad match," she went on.

"If he was faithful because of love, then it wasn't out of principle."

She smiled at him, and at that moment he reckoned she was nuts.

"That's exactly what Manfred always says, word for word."

Momo noticed the present tense, which made him feel uneasy. So what exactly was her conception of death? A corpse never enters into any conception. It's ashes or decay: there are no two ways about it. Already, right at the start, she'd said, "I cried, then calmed down. I now have another reason to go on living. So long as I think about him, he'll continue to be."

He was starting to get fed up with all this maternal philosophizing. What was her name again? Ah yes, Anna. He had seen her name in the report. Anna Michel. He stood up again, tried to unfold his body and felt the small of his back crack. He now found himself bent double, with a large fissure running through his coccyx.

"You don't take enough care of yourself. You need a massage."

Momo tried to straighten up, but the pain lingered. It would be like trying to iron out the folds in a piece of origami.

"Can I help you?"

"No thanks!"

He raised his arms, which soothed the pain a little. Anna kept staring at him with her large rectangular spearmint-green eyes.

"How wrong you are. One of these days, if you've got the time, I'll give you a massage. My hands are extremely effective."

Momo was starting to find her a little pushy and dotty. He pulled at his back. The cogs and wheels fleetingly discovered their usual connections. But the machinery itself was decidedly rusty. He filled his lungs with air, which made him cough with the raucous bark of a cigarillo-smoker coming home after running a race through a field of butts. It was a gargling mess of disgusting slimy mucous. Anna Michel waited for him to finish while staring at the *Pierrot le Fou* poster. When he'd finally stopped coughing his lungs up, her eyes were still fixed on the hard blueness at the centre of Belmondo's gob.

"Do you like that film?" she asked.

"It's a dream I could have had."

"For me, it's one of the few movies I've ever really enjoyed. I hate the cinema. It makes me sick. All I can stand are love poems like *Pierrot le Fou* or *Contempt* . . . Other films put me into a panic."

Momo thought this rather exaggerated. To be panicked by the cinema you really did need to be off your trolley and with a screw loose.

"I spent my childhood in Picardy in a tiny village, with a road-mender father and a handicapped mother. She'd caught polio before the war. I taught my own father to read and write. We didn't even have a TV set! Maybe that's why I'm incapable of enjoying films. I'm scared of the pictures. The first movie I saw at the school cinema club was a real nightmare. Hitchcock's *Vertigo*. I left the room after only fifteen minutes."

Momo couldn't take any more of this. This glass-blower was something from the Middle Ages. The spell had been broken, and he no longer found her in the slightest bit relaxing. He bent down to pick up a pair of dirty socks that were lying on the floor and then, to his horror, noticed that his woolly dressing gown had drifted open. Its belt was hanging down his sides. Little Jimmy and his two playmates were dangling beneath the camel's belly. He noticed the glassblower glance furtively at this tragic spectacle, then primly turn her eyes away. Momo closed his dressing gown once more while thinking about Belmondo trying to extinguish the fuse of dynamite at his feet at the end of *Pierrot le Fou*. He was sure that if he had been in the same situation right then, he would make no effort to put it out. It would be better to die in an explosion than of shame.

Jean-Paul Lefèvre, Commissioner Aline Lefèvre's former husband, emptied the bottle of Patrimonio into Maurice's glass.

"Same again, Toni!"

The Athena Bar had one of the most attractive ranges of terraces and piss artists of all the cafés on Place Saint-Nicolas in Bastia. On the floor tiles, the sawdust acted as both a spittoon and an ashtray. Being hundreds of miles away from Montmartre face to face with another Commissioner Lefèvre had a strange effect on Maurice. As soon as he had picked him up at the airport, the Corsican-Breton had pointed out: "But she did insist on keeping my name. She can say what she wants, but that really did matter!"

"The Suppinis have always had the evil eye. In each generation there's an 'unexplained' violent death. Anyway, you know what we're like. We don't explain things, we just react . . ."

The male version of Commissioner Lefèvre had apparently gone native and picked up a Bastia accent. The local plonk probably had something to do with it.

"In the 1950s the grandfather ran into a bullet one morning on a pavement in Neuilly and didn't even have time to say hello!"

"A settling of scores?"

"Here, the calculator and computer are recent discoveries. So the scores are still being reckoned up."

Lefèvre laughed raucously. His excessive wine

consumption gave him the dank breath of an old dog, and his laughter sounded like a steam train setting off.

"In the next generation of the Suppini family, it was her father. He was 'vanished' or more exactly 'vaporized' at the beginning of the 1980s. His wife says he left home one morning and was never seen again. But it wasn't to buy cigarettes, because he didn't even smoke. We don't know if he was killed or simply ran away to the other end of the earth, or even to Nice, Marseilles or Naples. It's a complete mystery. Now, twenty years later, it's his daughter. I tell you, it's the evil eye! Cheers!"

Momo clinked glasses once more. The wine was as thick as a girl's aperitif. The male Lefèvre could apparently take it, but he was going to have to go slowly. "Wine for the body and laughter for the soul" was a saying that had been dreamed up just for him. He was in his fifties, a bit wrecked, a little slimy, one of those ugly beauties that women adore, in the Serge Gainsbourg or Tom Waits category. Momo would easily have accepted putting on ten years if he could inherit such a ripened head of debauchery.

"So you reckon that Elsa could have been a settling of scores?"

"No, that isn't what I said at all!"

"OK, the evil eye, then . . ."

"It's just bad luck, that's all. Women are never victims of vendettas in Corsica. They have very strict rules here."

"But I suppose the grandfather didn't get his bullet just out of politeness."

"No, but the old boy was rolling in it. He owned half the garages on the eastern plain. After the war, people were still in the Middle Ages around here. The shopkeepers acted as bankers, lending money, acting as

guarantors and so on for distant cousins or the neighbours. They shook hands, then pledged their word: 'If
you act as my guarantor, I'll give you the orange grove,
or uncle's sheep fold.' Obviously, the system had certain drawbacks. When someone went out of business,
or died, the agreement wasn't always honoured. And
so, one morning, a bullet would bump into someone
on a pavement, lender or borrower, as the case might
be. Because of a mistake in how the deal had been
interpreted."

"So it was just a simple difference of opinion?"

"Exactly! Things are highly subtle here. You have to
read between the lines. A bigwig who turns up late at
the funeral of someone who's been shot is making an
important statement: he detested the dead man, he's
pleased he's gone and may even have had something
to do with his murder. But just try putting someone
away for turning up late for mass!"

The male Lefèvre emptied the second bottle of
Patrimonio. Momo could no longer feel the borders
of his skull or remember where he was exactly. The
bar, which was dark and smelly just like any other old
bar anywhere else in Europe, with its football tro-
phies and upside-down bottles, didn't look at all
Corsican.

"It's nice here," he lisped, lighting a cigarillo.

"A bar which is grimy out of principle, and not just
by chance!" the male Lefèvre replied proudly, as if he
were personally responsible for its condition. "The
owner insists on it! I mean, this isn't a hospital, is it? So
no one's allowed to sweep the floor!"

Once more, Momo pictured Elsa's face, her youth,
smile and determination. Bastia made that little ambitious virginal seamstress easier to fathom. And he also
grasped more fully what the sculptor on Rue Burcq

had said: "She gave the impression of having been through a lot."

"So women are never involved in Corsican business?"

"Of course they are! They encourage their men, make decisions, calm things down or else throw oil onto the fire. They sometimes even get into fights!"

"So it's a possibility?"

"But your kid wasn't involved in any fights."

Momo thought of Elsa during the strike at the Moulin Rouge. She hadn't hesitated about leading the struggle.

"But she was certainly no coward."

"She seems to have rather appealed to you, Inspector."

"What about the mother? What does she have to say about the disappearance of her husband? I mean, she was married to the girl's father, I suppose?"

"She doesn't say anything. She just crosses her fingers and talks about the evil eye."

"And you?"

"Rumours say that old man Suppini joined the ranks of the Mafia. It sometimes happens that the Italian godfathers let the Corsicans take a seat at the end of the row. Once every twenty years, so I'm told."

"Meaning?"

"The Corsicans and the Mafia have always helped each other out, even if the Corsicans have never really played a major role. But Corsica itself interests the Mafia. With good reason. It is the least populated, the least developed and best preserved region of the entire Mediterranean. And the reigning chaos here means they can impose whatever rules they like, through sheer muscle, while the state is still fumbling for its car keys. So it's an ideal place to launder money.

And the Mafia needs figureheads, and being a figure-head is an excellent career for a Corsican. But then, you come up against the same problem. If one day you start trying to figure too largely in the business, you won't necessarily have time to nod good day to your bullet. But that's all just rumours, if that! More like whispering... Here, the Mafia's called the 'Sea Breeze', because you can scarcely hear it, you can't see it, but from time to time it whips up one hell of a storm!"

"I have problems understanding how they make any money out of this shit-heap."

"Corsica is full of havens for the elite. The cream of European royalty and celebs have villas, palaces and yachts here. Ministers, TV stars, top models, in fact anyone you're likely to see on the cover of *Paris-Match*. And for their marvellous properties and private beaches, they pay extremely high rates. There's a revolutionary tax for you! In the end, it suits a lot of people that terrorist attacks mean that Corsica is no Costa Brava."

"So, according to you, the kid can't have been victim of some old story that started up here decades ago, concerning her granddad's pile. That's fine with me, but what I need is a clear answer. You know my boss better than I do, and she doesn't accept facile explanations. What I tell her has to stand up in court."

"Round here, nothing stands up in court. It's Ancient Greece. And I don't mean the same philosophy as Socrates, just Athens before Rome and before Jesus Christ. Tragedy, fraternal in-fighting, terrible revenge, women with faces of carved wood mourning their children. All kinds of gods, sun, translucent water, olive trees, cheese made of goat's milk and ewe's milk. It's incredible! The landlord of this very bar where we're getting pissed is no egghead, but he still organizes philosophical discussions and chess tournaments. One of the fishmongers in the market slaps up messages of wisdom in his shop window. And not your usual eye-catching stuff like 'forget your mother-in-law, buy a young trout'. No. Real intellectual stuff. He puts Sartre quotes up beside the price of red mullet: 'You would need a double sun to enlighten the depths of human stupidity.' And while he's gutting his mackerel and filleting his soles, he slags off people who don't read. It makes you think that Plato's about to spring out from behind the next orange tree, or that the statue of Homer's going to nod towards the sea."

All of this talk of the sea, Greece and Homer's statue reminded Momo of Jean-Luc Godard. And it was just a short step from *Contempt* to *Pierrot le Fou*, ugly Anna's favourite movie. His too. That was one point they had in common. He was going to see her again, that's what he'd told himself on the plane. But would he dare to? The Patrimonio red was going to his head. Corsica wasn't as he'd imagined it. There had been two terrorist attacks that night. One in Ajaccio against the Corsican Economic Development Agency, the other against the Tourism Bureau in Porto-Vecchio. As far as Momo was concerned, Napoleon's native island was just that – bombs and shit-heads, a Northern Ireland in the wrong sea with a Basque beret shoved under its armpit. He had been expecting to find a place that was gutted with explosives, its inhabitants creeping along the walls and trembling with fear, hardly daring to look at the blood-red sea or the hinterland which had been devastated by forest fires, but he had flown over a quiet postcard stuck up on a extremely blue lake by a permanent anticyclone. The sea was coloured like a bubble bath, with verdant trees parading down to it. The earth had been photographed then computer-enhanced. There were no two ways about it. Reality was a bad scenario with no twists or turns in its plot.

At the end of the second bottle of Patrimonio, Maurice asked if he could go to his hotel. It was eleven-thirty, and he needed a nap before lunchtime. He was already in a Southern mood. Jean-Paul Lefèvre gave him a lift.

"I'll leave you to think things over and take a look at the file. Apart from the usual business, we're onto an illegal trade in porno cassettes between Bastia and Italy. We've been watching them for months, and we're just about to round them up."

Maurice couldn't care less about the commissioner's concerns. He kept his eyes half closed against the blinding light that was bathing the semi-ruined, semi-magnificent Italianate houses. A violent mortal gleam that burned your eyes and the scrub while turning the sea into a slick of molten metal. At the heart of the Mediterranean, the sun was no longer a source of life and sweetness. It was the dark eye of death. Fascinated by this heavenly combustion, Maurice fell silent. The male Lefèvre made the most of the opportunity to deliver a few insights into life with the female Lefèvre.

"When you get dumped by a girl like that, you have to wait and see. Don't jump on the first thing in a bra. You get bored stiffless by all that pussy that's just after your milk. You want the one who dumped you, there's no way out of it. A thousand other lousy lays can only tell you one thing: run back to her! Too bad. Aline's not the sort of girl you can run back to as easily as that. If you beg, she guts you and before you know it, you're rolled and strung up like a roast in a supermarket freezer. So I said to myself: calm down my lad and tighten your belt, that's the only way you're ever going to get to her."

"And did it work?"

"If a car doesn't move, its battery goes flat. If you stop monkeying with your libido, it'll let go of your balls!"

"I'm afraid that's something I'm not paid to know about. Otherwise I'd be in the top tax bracket."

"What? You too! You also ran up against a rock?"

"With me, it's more like bad luck, followed by a lack of interest. If you don't take wing, you don't crash-land."

"In my generation, of course, we experienced the wonders of the 1970s. Back then you didn't need to put on the dog to get some tail."

That tormented face, with its teeth eaten away by tobacco and its bleary eyes, burst out laughing. Things got moving again.

"When I think that we should soon be able to stop tormenting our groins, and now they're inflicting Viagra on us! It's just too much!"

Momo took his case out of the boot. He was all in.

"I'll pick you up in an hour, and we'll go and have a bite to eat. Then I'll drop you off where the kid's mother lives. She'll be expecting you at three. By the way, for your information, do you know what 'tragedy' means in Ancient Greek?"

"I didn't even do any Latin, so it's all Greek to me."

"*Trag-oedia*, or tragedy, means 'goat song'!"

Maurice Laice wondered if this false Corsican was talking about him. He had never set foot in Greece, knew nothing about the tragedies of Sophocles and Euripides, but he certainly stank like an old goat and sang just as badly.

In his room, he lay down fully dressed on the flowery quilt and flicked through the file Lefèvre had given him. It contained a stack of notes and reports about the grandfather's and father's disappearances and about their more or less official links with members of the Corsican Liberation Front. Was there much point in chopping down any more trees for this? What could he do except provide tons of paperwork to satisfy the ravenous maw of the female Lefèvre? *Sea Breeze, Movement for Autodetermination, A Cuncolta, the legal wing of the Corsican Liberation Front, The Canal Historique* . . . All of it skated around without forming any coherent figures along with the Patrimonio, which was boiling away merrily in his brains. Nothing doing. He had lost his sense of rhythm. He thought of Anna, Manfred's aged and ugly mother. She was pear-shaped, with extremely narrow shoulders and hips like a pre-Columbian statue. But he'd ended up forgetting that she was old and plain. Her eyes took up a lot of space. He just couldn't imagine her in her workshop in Beauvais. A glassblower? How could she do that with such narrow shoulders? She'd been ill, her son had been murdered, but still she didn't collapse in a heap. No. She didn't even cry. She whispered, staring straight ahead. In the end, he'd worked out why her eyes took up so much room. You had to be near death to see things clearly and stop seeing the world in the beam of a Maglite.

Momo pictured his mother in that narrow beam. He called her at once. Got his thoughts together. He had to be strong, and comforting.

"I'm off to Toulouse to see your cousin Julie," she explained in a firm voice. "I need a change of air."

Momo didn't like that. So his mother was going to see her niece in Toulouse for a change of air? When you travel, you take your brains with you, and the air you breathe can't make much difference.

"So I can't come and see you?"

"When?"

"I don't know . . . I'm in Corsica right now."

"See? You've always got other things to do!"

"I'll come as soon as I can."

"Anyway, you've got Julie's number, haven't you?"

The silence lengthened. Momo felt that he was no longer capable of even speaking to his mother, or of talking her round. He was a real coward. She sounded worried:

"Is something the matter?"

Momo shut up. Why did he always turn things arse about face? He was supposed to be protecting his mother, not the other way round. Here she was, going off her rocker and there was nothing he could do about it. To perk him up a bit, she said:

"Life goes on, you know."

Maurice Laice was speechless. He wondered if it had ever even begun for him.

Clutching a map like a tourist, Momo wandered through the old quarter of Bastia, perched on its citadel. Mysterious scraps of conversation echoed between the cool damp walls. Its peeling buildings with their worm-eaten window frames and clothes hung out to dry made him feel as if he was in Naples. He went up a stairway into a dead-end street. This was more reminiscent of Montmartre. He felt nauseous. The male Lefèvre had stuffed him with charcuterie and stewed boar. Various beasts were fighting it out in his intestinal arena, with a violence heightened by the Patrimonio red. He could have swallowed two bottles of Badoit in one go. In the dark dirty apartment where Elsa's mother lived, Momo had found a photo of the little seamstress with her friend Carla Cristofari on the beach at Lumio, just before she'd gone up to the capital. Her mother, dressed in black, her face a craggy cliff set with bloodshot eyes, swore that the murderers were madmen from over *there*, who had nothing to do with her little girl over *here*. She kept on stroking the head of her black dog, a large mongrel whose constituent parts Momo was incapable of identifying. Only this large placid animal seemed to interest her. As a dressmaker, she had taught her daughter to snip, assemble and sew. She was now unemployed, scraping by on the dole. Distant, distrustful, worn out by the tragedies that had now left her on her own, she never let go of her pet's fur except to cross her fingers against the evil eye.

In Elsa's room Momo got to know the ambitious little Corsican girl a little better. There was a fragrance of vibrant youth, something between musk and vanilla. Clothes impregnated with a brunette's spice. A photobooth snap of her at the age of thirteen. Alain Bashung records. A signed poster of Enzo Enzo. A few sentences written in a slender hand on a sheet of blue paper: *I design men's clothes because I need to picture solid limbs, flat stomachs, furry chests, high buttocks, the swelling of an organ between the legs . . . Success and wealth do not bring happiness, but raising yourself up removes self-loathing. The other idiots think I am fragile. They are too full of themselves to notice the energy that will avenge my existence. I'll make up reasons to be here . . . I have a future, I've been sure of that ever since I was little. One day, I'll look due south with all of Paris at my feet. A man will embrace me, licking my clitoris* . . . Momo had jumped. This was a virgin talking? It all rang false. But the mother confirmed that it was her daughter's writing. Awaiting illumination, Momo stayed for a long time in her room. He would so have liked to have seen her sewing brocades, adjusting them on a model, folding back the stitches of a hem, raising up a collar, stepping back to take a good look at her work. He pictured her placing her forehead against the cold glass of the only window in her tiny bedsit to stare at the wall of the building opposite, cloudy with grime, just like the perimeter of a prison, with occasional gloomy windows cutting the rusty roughcast. Maurice slid into her dreams, rising up with her into a universe of taffeta and cashmere to "remove self-loathing", as she put it on her blue notepaper. Murderers also kill intimacy, and Momo was fed up with his part as a mole. But at least he now had a better understanding of the energy Elsa had put into fleeing this sordid apartment and that shrivelled woman she had as a mother, with a face that had solidified into a tragic mask, maybe from Greece itself. It had been with no regret that Momo had left her. She hadn't taught him anything much. But she had agreed to give him some information about Carla Cristofari, Elsa's childhood friend, a folksinger who lived in the old quarter of Bastia.

Momo was impatient to see this Carla on her perch at the top of the citadel. But the ascent of old Bastia was hard going, and Maurice was now coughing his lungs up.

He went into the crumbling building, which must have been beautiful once, with its majestically wide staircase. On the second floor Carla opened the door, appearing as lovely as she was in the photo on the beach at Lumio, with slate-grey eyes and painted mouth against the smooth white of her face. He'd imagined that she would be more bulky. She looked too delicate to be a Corsican folksinger. She was dressed in black, a miniskirt above her dark tights, large Doc Martens and a V-neck sweater that hinted at the nakedness of her round breasts. She had a cigarette in her mouth. Momo's heart pounded to see her there, just like that, so beautiful, so young, like a surviving part of Elsa.

"Sorry, I thought . . ."

"I'm the one who's sorry. I'm from the police. I'm here to talk to you about your friend Elsa Suppini."

She cleared her throat with an over-loud cough, then froze in such perfect stillness that it appeared contrived. Momo thought of Jean-Paul Lefèvre's hobbyhorse: that Corsica was Greece, and realized that this girl looked a bit like a young Melina Mercouri.

Maurice attempted a smile for her and, for once, felt like he'd succeeded.

"Can I come in?"

"Please do."

She was clearly not as pleased as all that, but she had no choice and didn't like it one bit. Momo headed for the only door in the room. It led to what was both the bathroom and toilet. The window was open; Maurice leaned out and saw a man, or a boy more like, standing on a cornice before jumping onto a balcony and vanishing amid the maze of roofs. Momo had no desire to die falling from a high building in Corsica, so he went back to the girl, still with his engaging smile, which he still found successful, if a little fixed. He stubbed out the Chesterfield that was smoking in the ashtray and put his smile to rest. He thought of Anna, fleetingly, almost tenderly. How she had managed to ask him: "Why do you like yourself so little?"

"You can explain the basics to your pal. First, don't make so much noise. Second, don't forget to put out your cigarette. He might have a head for heights, but he made such a din that he gave you a cough. Something tells me he doesn't want to say hello, which isn't very polite. Who is he?"

"A friend."

"Jean-Baptiste Monetti?"

The name panicked her. How did he know?

"Elsa's 'fiancé', the one she dumped before going to Paris?"

"Yes," the pretty brunette murmured.

"The neighbours of the Suppinis say that they had quite a row just before Elsa left for the capital. Jean-Baptiste is supposed to have threatened her, to have said that some day or other she'd pay for what she'd done."

"He was just upset! Jean-Baptiste wouldn't hurt a fly. He was really in love with Elsa, but she was so . . ."

She broke off, stubbed out her cigarette, then curled herself up in an armchair. With her arms folded over her stomach, she looked like a little girl. Momo suddenly realized that he'd never have any children. What was up with him? Something was inching its way inside him, turning him into a softy. He couldn't help it, he just wanted to protect this girl. He finished her sentence for her:

"She was so strong-headed, is that it? So ambitious?"

"She wanted to gobble up the entire world!"

"What were you doing on the day of the murder?"

She went over to a small desk beside the window, then handed Maurice an article that had appeared in the *Corse-Matin* the day after Elsa's death. It told of Carla Cristofari's performance at the theatre of Porto Vecchio the previous evening. Her airy voice, the intensity of her presence, the audience's emotions: the journalist had been less struck by the magic of the singer than the grace of her words. A rather hazy photo showed the slender performer, wearing a short black dress, in a pallid halo of light. Momo thought of the male Lefèvre's ridiculous obsession with Greek tragedy and it froze his blood. He stood up, took a long look at the CD rack, then handed a disc to Carla.

"I'd like to hear you. May I?"

She obeyed. On the wall, a poster advertising a festival in Calvi contained a barely recognizable depiction of her, with an airbrushed blue-tinted face. He pictured her singing a cappella in a chapel choir, in the courtyard of a building, on the stage of a theatre. Her voice rose up, powerful, slightly throaty, as though amplified by the nave of a cathedral. A beautifully pure sound that slipped beneath his skin, causing it to become unwrinkled and swell up with emotion.

"And don't you want to gobble up the world too?"

"I don't have much appetite."

Momo avoided looking at her. Her lack of appetite moved him. She was like him! Except that she was lucky enough to be a singer. He stopped himself from telling her that she was young, that she still had enough time to overcome her fears.

"I've never been able to chase away my fears," she said, as though reading his thoughts. "That's why I admired Elsa."

"What about your Jean-Baptiste? It's not very smart to run away from a police officer like that."

"I suppose he didn't feel like having anything to do with someone from the mainland."

"You reckon Corsicans are any better?"

"No, just different."

"He's already done time, hasn't he?"

She looked at him, the word "yes" refusing to emerge from her mouth.

"You know that's hardly a big revelation, Carla. I could find out right away."

Pronouncing her name made him feel good. He would have liked to tell her that he wasn't there to bug her, even though it certainly looked that way. He'd had enough of being hated, especially by her. It was as though Elsa was freezing him out.

"He wasn't even twenty at the time. A hold-up that went wrong."

"And he's already out and about? Things can't have gone as wrong as all that."

Maurice felt awful faced with this girl, curled up on herself, her voice singing of the melancholic wonders of the world. But he couldn't stand little crooks like

Jean-Baptiste. What were these two girls doing with such a jerk? He'd had it with two-bit thugs blessed with the glittering aura of being bandits. He asked Carla about Manfred and about the sculptor on Rue Burcq. She told him that she'd never heard of them. Elsa had only been back to Bastia once, at Christmas. Carla had seen her, but the young go-getter hadn't confided in her at all. All she'd spoken about was her projected collection of clothes.

"She said that she'd met someone, but it was all highly mysterious. I never found out who it was. She said that she'd soon come back to Corsica with him . . ."

Momo knew that Elsa had been fortunate enough to believe in her dreams. Love is just a fantasy. A succession of bubbles to play with until they pop, leaving only a drop of water. By meticulously gathering each drop of this tiny manna, some lucky bastards might just about fill up a small glass before they die. Life was just that patient collection of the water of dreams, the sole nectar of existence.

"Did Elsa know that you and Jean-Baptiste were together?"

"She didn't care. Jean-Baptiste never meant that much to her."

She sounded reproachful. Elsa was the sort who looked down on her fellows, who wanted to breathe a different air, to enjoy a more delightful life, and who flung their desires into other people's faces. Carla pouted adorably. Momo was smitten. It seemed to him that this brunette also looked like the dead girl in his arms, asphyxiated by a water heater. It was the model around which all his possible loves circulated.

"I'm going to have to report the fact that your Jean-Baptiste ran away. He's now a wanted man, which is dumb if it's just that he can't stand Parisians. Anyway, he can explain all that to his compatriots."

"But he hasn't done anything!"

Her voice was pleading. He stared into her eyes. He would have given anything to make her trust him, which was unthinkable. Even he would not have granted himself such a privilege. He knew himself too well for that.

"I don't know about your Jean-Baptiste. But as for you, I'm sure you had nothing to do with the murder of Elsa. I'm not supposed to tell you that, but from time to time even a cop has the right to believe in someone."

She smiled at him. He bore away that smile, convinced that he'd see her again some time, and that she'd trust him. He left her to her songs, which he could still hear down in the courtyard, echoing like hope imprisoned between the walls.

At the station, the male Lefèvre was in a fine state. He'd launched his roundup of the porno cassette merchants he'd had under surveillance for months. Momo was treated to the tale of his exploits while he drove him to the airport.

"Bastia has become the crossroads between America and Eastern Europe for pornography ferried via Italy, which is almost within spitting distance. The wops have set up a little underground production plant in a house in Cap Corse to copy videocassettes and print covers. Now all we have to do is take a look at them all to see what is and isn't legal. We should contact a few sperm banks. What with the amount of wanking this is going to trigger off, we ought to set up a system of recycling."

Momo shrugged.

"What about my kid? And her ex?"

"Monetti?"

The male Lefèvre had plenty on Jean-Baptiste, who had been a member of a dissident wing of the Corsican Liberation Front. He'd been caught during a hold-up that had been intended to fund his group, in other words to pay for the leaders' four-wheel drives. He hadn't stayed behind bars very long, presumably because it had been decided in high places that he knew too much and might cause problems for certain bigwigs.

"When was that?"

"Two years back."

"A few months before Elsa left for Paris?"

"And more importantly, shortly after the assassination of the Prefect. An exquisite corpse, as they say in Sicily."

"Sorry?"

"That's what they call certain people who've been wiped out by the Mafia. Deaths that suit everyone. That marvellous irreproachable man's murder was good news for the terrorists, the Mafia and the French state."

Lefèvre's car was motionless, stuck in the early-evening jam. They were in a suburban wasteland. No more sea, no more Neapolitan architecture. Maurice Laice wondered for a moment if he hadn't dreamed up Carla, the citadel and the religious chanting.

"How does Jean-Baptiste fit into all this?"

"Just tell me who decided that he was less dangerous out than inside. It's a mystery." The commissioner grimaced.

"What does he do for a living?"

"He's a studio director at the local TV station. A small salary and not much responsibility. It's a cushy number. A secure job and no headaches."

"Why did he run away?"

"An outsider and a cop in the same pair of pants is a bit too much for a little hood like him. He must have reckoned that you don't speak the same language and that it's better not to start up a conversation. I went through the same thing. Now it's sorting itself out. I've gone native. I had no choice. If you keep stuffing yourself with boar's meat, you start to grow bristles."

"All the same, we'll have to see if he was working the day Elsa was killed and check that he wasn't in Pigalle."

"I already have."

Momo was sick to death of his pregnant pauses. He felt like winding this former Breton up a bit.

"And?"

"And he'd taken a few days' leave."

"Jesus Christ!"

"Don't jump to conclusions. We'll pick him up soon enough. In the meantime, we'll have a little chat with his kith and kin."

"Anyway, I can't hang about lapping up your sea breezes till you grab him. You'll do the job better than me. I'm going back to report to the boss."

While they were having a farewell drink at the sparkling bright metal bar in the airport, the male Lefèvre had a special request:

"Don't tell my wife I talked to you about her. You know what she's like."

Sure enough, Momo clearly remembered his boss and was now wondering why she'd sent him out here. So he could get to know her ex? So as to have a free hand back in Montmartre? He thought of the man who'd had his throat ripped out on Rue Gerpil. Crack, synthetic drugs and real estate . . . What did Elsa, Carla and Jean-Baptiste have to do with all that? At first glance, nothing.

When he boarded the plane, all he had left was

Carla's smile. And the memory of Anna's eyes. Anna. Like Anna Karina in *Pierrot le Fou.* That hadn't occurred to him before.

They're drawing away. She can hear their voices. She's scared. She's scared that sobs will start racking her body despite herself and give her away. Tears can kill. Her guts, her chest and her throat hold them back, but the flood has to spill out somewhere. Her body is throbbing with pain. She dares to open her eyes. A cloud passes over her. She begs it to help her, to fill itself with her own rainwater. She hears them coming back, her legs shake, they're going to see how life persists inside her, beneath the bloody corpse that is protecting her. She closes her eyes. She doesn't budge. They are coming nearer. She hopes that the cloud has taken away enough tears so that nothing overflows.

From his window, Maurice Laice watched the comings and goings on Rue Doudeauville while nibbling at his thumbnail and sucking at his cigarillo. That made for a lot of pacifiers. During his absence Caty, the bureaucratic mouse, had examined the identities of the various owners of apartments on Rue Gerpil. One name cropped up more often than any other among the shareholders of the real-estate companies: a certain Pasquier, whose biography the ever-prolific Caty was now writing. Meanwhile, they still didn't have the slightest clue that might solve the murders at the Moulin Rouge. Momo hadn't made any progress at all since the bodies had been discovered. Neither in Corsica, nor in Paris. He jumped:

"So, Inspector, two days away from Montmartre and you're homesick already?"

Aline Lefèvre had silently entered his office. How long had the silly bitch been spying on him?

"You could have remained there longer. How domesticated can you get?"

Her face was puffy, and her eyes like glass. She must have been out partying again with her darling from the Ministry of Finance, plus some skirt they'd picked up in a nightclub. Momo produced a large cloud of cigarillo smoke just to piss her off. He thought of the male Lefèvre. He missed that fake Corsican and his head-piercing plonk. To avoid his boss's stare, he started fiddling with things on his desk.

"Turning myself into luggage gets on my nerves. How anyone can get off on such a ridiculous activity as travelling beats me."

"Don't mention getting off on anything, Inspector; it will only get you down."

"If you weren't my boss, I'd ask you what the difference is between you and a mosquito."

"I suppose it's that mosquitoes only bug you in the summer?"

"And now you don't even let me finish my own jokes."

"Anyway, will you please tell me about the terrible time you had far away from your precious Montmartre?"

"There isn't much to tell."

"Come on now, More is Less, don't make me kneel down and beg. Spit it out. I'm sure you've got something mentally prepared, ready to reel off by heart."

Momo told her about Jean-Baptiste, his CV, the way he legged it, then Carla and her local fame as a folk-singer. Apparently the boss liked what she was hearing.

"So it wasn't such a bad idea to send you over there. The local boys put in minimum hours!"

That wasn't particularly nice for her ex, and Momo refrained from dropping the wino any further in the shit. The phone rang. He at once recognized the fake Corsican's voice and so was careful about relaying that piece of information to the party-girl, who would have immediately told him to turn on the loudspeaker.

"You're not going to believe this, Inspector. I had to drink an entire bottle of Patrimonio after seeing it. I warn you, you won't like what I'm going to tell you. Your Snow White wasn't the sweet little angel you told me she was."

"I'm hanging on your every word. Are you going to give me enough rope?"

"I'll send you a package via one of our boys who's going to Paris. He'll drop it off at the station tomorrow noon at the latest."

"You couldn't give me a preface first?"

"I'd rather it was an after-word. We picked up the object in question during our raid in Cap Corse."

"I see."

"Not yet you haven't! Call me when you have . . . and not a word to my ex for the moment."

"Of course not."

He hung up. The female Lefèvre was observing him.

"What did he have to say?"

"Who?"

"Why, my ex of course."

"It was a friend of mine, a bookseller. Someone's asked him for some biographical information about Carco."

"I want you to phone up Lefèvre in Bastia every day to shake him up a bit."

"OK."

"As for the ground floor apartment on Rue Gerpil where you found the corpse, Caty is finding it heavy going. The ownership is being disputed, and Pasquier's lawyer is handling the case. I asked her to sketch out a plan of the entire building showing who owns what. She went there to investigate and found quite a crew. A gang of dealers, transvestites and whores just three hundred yards from the Théâtre des Abbesses."

Momo yawned loudly.

"That's Paris for you."

"If you were banking on an early night, think again. I'm going to need you this evening."

She explained her fucked-up scheme. A thief had squealed on a restaurant-owner on Rue Garraud who was running a home-delivery drug trafficking service on the side. She wanted to catch him red-handed that very night.

"But I really must concentrate on the Moulin Rouge murders," Momo pleaded.

He almost added that Carla now mattered to him. Finding the little dressmaker's murderer was the only way to chase away the obsessive dream of those two little Corsicans who had been smiling at him tenderly ever since he'd seen the photo of them on the beach in Lumio. Maurice had sworn to earn Carla's trust. That folksinger was a living version of Elsa. He was going to protect her from the actions of a friend who had wanted a fast and full life. Maybe because she'd sensed that it was all going to finish too soon in a theatrical bloodbath.

"There might even be a link between the throat victim on Rue Gerpil and the stiffs in the Moulin Rouge," the female Lefèvre went on stubbornly. "Rue Garraud lies directly between the two places, doesn't it?"

"I don't see any connection between your restaurateur and my two pin-ups."

"Want to bet?"

"Never."

"Stop being stubborn, More is Less. I don't trust the Drug Squad one bit. They've always got a little dealer somewhere ready to inform on a bigger fish, so they won't move until they know they're going net some barracuda in Bogota who moves dope by the ton."

Irritation was biting into her face, rounding her shoulders; she seemed to be rapidly approaching meltdown. Momo decided to drop the subject. She didn't.

"I've had enough of them congratulating themselves because crack hasn't caught on over here as much as it has in the States, because they managed to clean up the Stalingrad neighbourhood and reduce dealing to the eighteenth and Saint-Denis. There's not enough corpses for us to bother about any more!"

"Still going on about synthetic drugs," Momo sighed. "I'm sure your restaurant-owner isn't pushing angel dust or ecstasy."

"Even if he isn't, which you can't be sure of, he may well put me on another track . . ."

"Is this a CD you're playing?"

"Listen, Inspector, I'm fed up with you pissing on my parade all the time. Shit in little pills may well be less inspiring than the adventures of romantic poets and opium addicts in the Golden Triangle. But a girl who wakes up in Berkeley the day after a party and finds herself covered with the sperm of the five little fuckers who spiked her cola . . . Well, to be perfectly frank, I think it's no laughing matter."

Momo stared at her, then lit a cigarillo. He wasn't sure what all this was about. He'd never mingled sperm with his school pals. She was looking away from him. It was her turn to examine the window. He suddenly wondered if he now understood her obsession with designer drugs and hatred of the male sex.

"I was nineteen," she said softly. "And it certainly didn't inspire me to explore male sexuality with any interest or enthusiasm. It's not my fault if the smell of testosterone doesn't exactly turn me on."

She'd said it now. Momo didn't know what to do with himself. He now knew why she was so obsessed with these new drugs. He thought of Carla, who was counting on him, and of Anna, who had talked to him. Of all the dead who led him towards more women. Victims. All the same, he was no bastard: more of a zero, less than nothing. He told her he was sorry; she left his office, dryly saying over her shoulder:

"This evening, at ten, in front of Pigall's."

Momo left the station in a filthy mood. He'd had enough of it! The weather was still spring fresh, in other words icy cold, with a breeze fit to rip your teeth out. The African vibes on Rue Doudeauville soothed his nerves even before he reached Rue Poulet. He thought of Anna, who he still hadn't phoned. After all, she had suggested a massage. "One day, you'll see; you'll relax and feel as good as new. I've got hands of steel." He might believe in the strength of her hands, but he couldn't believe in any renaissance for him. But maybe faith would come during the process. That woman might stop him from becoming a complete misogynist, which would be a good thing. He didn't like the idea that one day he might realize that he had to turn towards partners with members. It would be hard at his age to put up with such a turnabout. Apparently, there are loads of men in the closet, not daring to come out. What was up with him? Momo could hardly see himself getting it up for some hairy muscleman or callow youth. He mentally prepared an explanation: "My boss, despite being a woman, is a crazed masochist, and I'm frightened I'll start being a total sexist . . ." No, he wouldn't dare. He'd simply ask her out to dinner, to apologize for the poor hospitality at his place.

He was feeling almost merry when he dialled her number. Joy was never a lasting emotion for him, but there was no answer. He wondered if she'd already gone back to Beauvais. No. She'd said that she'd stay for a while to sort out Manfred's things. Momo tried to remember her voice. It was slightly hoarse, very deep, almost pained. She always spoke in a hush, as if everything she said was in confidence, and the thought of it moved him.

He pushed open the door of L'Oracle, pleased to see Boualem's friendly features suggesting a beef and carrot stew, which had simmered all night along with a veal bone.

"It's like butter!"

Sure enough, it melted between the tongue and palate. Momo savoured his only moment of well-being that evening. Boualem mentioned the man who'd had his throat ripped out on Rue Germain Pilon. Momo pursed his lips

"The boss reckons it's about dope. She's got a score to settle. Plus she's looking into the possibility of a real-estate scam."

"Not bad! Do you know the difference in price between Avenue Junot and the roads going down to Pigalle? Double and sometimes even triple! The day things start levelling out, some people are going to be rolling in it."

"In the meantime, I have no desire to freeze my arse off in Pigalle this evening . . ."

"Try a slice of Pont-L'évêque. It's in fine fettle right now and will keep you on your feet."

Momo went for it. It was a cheese he hadn't eaten since leaving Normandy. A Granville madeleine. He thought of the Channel as it constantly came and went, of the soothing confusion of misty, blurry, indefinite objects, of those ever-shifting eternal frontiers between the earth, the sea and the sky.

"Maybe your boss has got it wrong," Boualem went on. "In fact, she definitely has, because things are always worse than they seem."

He looked devastated. Momo had never seen him like this before.

"Why are you interested in all this?"

"Professional curiosity."

"You're a psychiatrist now?"

Boualem sat down in front of him. Momo fell silent.

"I was a cop, Maurice. A cop just like you."

Momo stared at him in disbelief. Boualem looked awful.

"A fucking cop!"

"In Algiers?"

"Yes. I tried to make myself scarce, but it wasn't easy."

Momo silently stared at his glass. He wasn't sure if he really wanted to hear Boualem's confidences, but it was too late now. The Algerian had decided to talk, and Momo was shaking already. Boualem's voice was barely audible:

"The father opened the door. 'Are you Fouad Benmehdi?' The man said yes and then got shot in the chest. We were sent off like that after a simple tip-off. An anonymous letter led to someone getting executed. We took uppers to stay awake. We couldn't stand it any more. The situation lasted for years. One day, one of my colleagues got seriously wounded. The boss just said: 'So what? You're paid to die.' One night, the patrol car got caught up in a shoot-out. A bullet took my shoulder off. The guy next to me was dead. I leaned over him and closed my eyes. We stayed like that until seven the next morning."

Momo's throat was burning. Boualem in the arms of a corpse. Apparently, there was no escaping it!

"One day, I cracked. I refused to fire during a raid. So I rotted for a year in jail. I don't know why they didn't kill me. I suppose they must have been planning on using me. For an entire year all I thought about was food. I learned recipes and invented others. It gave me the hope that one day I'd get out of that shit-hole and then live life as a pure gourmet, to start all over again, from zero."

Momo knocked back his glass in one. Boualem and his culinary skills, his good mood, his agility and attentiveness . . . a cop!

"No one knows, Maurice. I just try to survive without being bothered. I avoid seeing my fellow expatriates. They have too many horror stories to tell. Like me, they still turn around when they're walking in the street, because they're scared. Whole villages were wiped out, do you realize that? You can never forget that, you no longer know what being calm and easy means, you're ashamed to be alive. I read newspapers now. I devour their never really true stories. And I try to understand."

"Boualem, the bill for table three please!" the boss yelled.

Pale and trembling, Boualem slowly stood up. He wasn't waltzing around any more. Momo stayed there frozen for a moment, then dragged himself out of that old bistro. His body felt terribly heavy.

From Place Pigalle, he swayed along the boulevard, which he'd always considered to be a moat around the Montmartre castle of his childhood. It was cold. Luckily, the beef and carrots and the Pont-L'évêque were doing their calorific work. What was more, after Boualem's little tale, Momo could no longer really complain about his easy beat as a public servant. It was practically a hobby! He came to a halt at the corner of Rue Houdon. It stank of car fumes. The neon lights and signs of the sex shops were spilling their fluorescent colours into the darkness, amid the eyes of the cars and the gleams of the lampposts. He ordered a strong espresso at Au Bar des Artistes while observing the exit of the club over the road. While he was stirring his coffee, his mobile rang. It was Caty, the little mouse:

"Are you ready? She'll be out in five minutes. She's just been to the cloakroom, and now she's powdering her nose."

Momo gave up scalding his tongue and put down his coffee. It seemed that womankind had been designed to piss him off. He crossed to the left corner, taking up position in front of the door of Pigall's, beneath the awnings of a lesbian club offering erotic songs and readings. Two girls went inside, intertwined. On the door, which swung shut heavily, a poster explained: "A woman has 228 erogenous zones. So does a man." Two approximate drawings depicted a naked man and woman. Around the woman, 228 arrows pointed all over her body, forming a gigantic forest of acupuncture. The man also got 228 arrows, but all aimed at one single point: his penis. Maurice was in no mood to smile; he cursed instead. How terrible this feminist-cum-lesbian fury was! He congratulated himself for abandoning any form of sexual activity. The twenty-first century would be the age of wanking or it would be nothing at all.

Momo turned round. This was no time to start philosophizing. The girl had slipped out and was now by the fountain on Place Pigalle. He walked around it. She went down Rue Coustou, then vanished into number 4. He waited, leaning against the opposite porch, hiding in the shadows, trying to warm himself up by smoking a cigarillo. The cold was giving him backache. He was shaking like a pneumatic drill. Would he ever be warm again? He had a vivid vision of his father's face, his gnarled hands and hunched figure. Dead, totally dead! Most of the time, he managed to forget. His father, rooted in the earth. But the slightest blast of cold brought back the old boy's face, and all Momo could think about was the cemetery now waiting for him. To get it over with, to finish this process that starts at birth. His mobile's ringing tone pulled him out of this morbid train of thought. This time it was the boss:

"The order was put through twenty minutes ago. The guy's just left Place Emile-Goudot on a scooter."

Momo was ready. He could hear the whirr of the machine, waited till the man had parked, then crept up behind him silently just at the moment when he was entering the entry code. The lad looked round at him in a panic. Momo nodded, as if saying hello, let him go in and went up the stairs behind him. His lungs were aching. Jesus, he was definitely going to die before his time and never benefit from his pension. When the lad rang on a bell on the fifth floor, Momo pretended to go up to the sixth, very slowly, until the door opened, then he rushed in, card in his hand, gun in the lad's guts, yelling "Police!"

He could already hear the siren downstairs. The cops were clambering up faster than he had done. They were all fit from training. The lad had three grams of coke on him. In Momo's mobile, Aline Lefèvre was triumphant: handcuffs were now stopping the owner of the restaurant on Rue Garroud from scratching his arse. Momo sometimes used to go for a bite there. He was from the Auvergne and, in terms of cuisine, produced Chinese, French and North African dishes. There's nothing wrong with being cosmopolitan. How could he avoid thinking of Boualem, whose livelihood depended on his palate?

It had started raining again. Momo slowly climbed up the slope towards the Butte, then stopped at the corner of Rue Lepic to have a last drink. Back at Rue Gabrielle, his pit was looking more and more as though it was unfit for human habitation. He slumped down fully clothed on his damp bed.

It seemed like several minutes passed, then he heard, at a great distance, the ring of his mobile. He'd slept like a log. It was already eight in the morning, and the male Lefèvre was calling.

"Admit it, Inspector," the fake Corsican intoned. "You were worried I'd have nothing to do with your case, and now you'd rather I got off it."

"Get to the point, Lefèvre. I'm in a coma here."

"It's about your fugitive, Jean-Baptiste Monetti. Guess what he was up to on the day your little darling was murdered."

"You son of a bitch, stop calling her that!"

"That's not very nice."

"Come on, out with it."

"Hanging around in bars comes in handy. A hack on *Corse-Matin* told me that your Jean-Baptiste was playing a friendly football match against Sartène on the day in question. He's part of the team of journalists."

Momo closed his eyes, trying to weigh up the importance of the news. He was relieved that it wasn't the kid who had wiped out Manfred and Elsa. It was better for Carla.

"He isn't a journalist, but he works for television. You noticed how fast he runs, which is a strong point in a footballer."

"Send me a report. The boss needs something concrete, and we're rushed off our feet right now."

"I'll fax you. Anyway, I'll bet you phone me back once you've taken a look at what I've sent you. And don't take it too much to heart – your romantic side will be the death of you."

Momo drank his coffee while it was still too hot. He hated that, but he was late. The boss must already be waiting for him. They now had to trawl their way through the Auvergnat's address book. Maurice couldn't stop yawning. The very idea of fish made him seasick.

It had been a very bad idea of Aline Lefèvre's to search the homes of the Auvergnat's customers, the restaurateur who delivered dope to homes like others did pizzas, within an hour of the call. "You dreamed it was possible, the Auvergnat makes your dreams come true!" Whatever had the commissioner been thinking of? The Auvergnat had been no Mafia dealer, laundering millions through the Crédit Lyonnais. He supplied small doses for immediate consumption that very evening. So there were no big fish to be found among his clientele, and you had to be simple-minded to think there would be. What did Aline Lefèvre have between her ears? Only hot air?

"You see? There is a link between my restaurateur and your lovebirds in the Moulin Rouge!"

Sure enough, Momo had searched the apartments of two dancers from the cabaret, whose names appeared in the Auvergnat's address book. He'd rifled through drawers full of panties and bras without finding a single leaf of grass. Just some dildos and vibrators, which led Momo to a few consoling reflections. Were such beauties also reduced to mechanizing their libido? Apparently, no one can fuck you better than yourself! Or maybe the partners of these girls, as perfect as an adolescent's wet dream, weren't up to it, and their members lacked the necessary gradient? In any case, when faced with the dizzy heights of sex, it was better to get yourself automated than resort to

108

Viagra, which was so dangerous for the ticker. Momo felt less lonely.

"I don't call that a link. It's more like a blank. I don't see any reason to rejoice."

"The samples of medicine we found there haven't been analysed yet. And some of those pills look decidedly iffy to me."

"I don't like this sort of hunt. I'm more of a gatherer."

"Ever since Cro-Magnon man, that's hardly been a sign of advanced civilization."

Momo sighed. He had methodically been through all their boxes of pills, had removed a tablet from each packet that wasn't still sealed. This was hardly going to win him a medal! He yawned. It was five in the afternoon, and he was fed up. He thought again about the package that the male Lefèvre had promised to send him that morning.

"I have to go and see if there's any news from Corsica," he said.

He went to reception to see the secretary and the orderly. The parcel hadn't arrived. So Momo worked on his reports covering the lad on the moped and the dancing girls. Caty dropped in to throw her smile into his face while explaining that the girls weren't on police records. They were clean as can be.

Momo nodded in what was supposed to be an encouraging way. The kid should have been a bureaucrat instead. In irritation, he plunged his incisor into his Caran d'Ache HB pencil, penetrating as far as its lead. Just pray the mouse went on typing away at her keyboard and going online or whatever. Meanwhile, she wasn't burdening him with her smiles.

"And what have you found out about the properties on Rue Gerpil?"

"Pasquier's CV is coming on nicely. I'll probably need another day or two to find out everything, but he's got shares in an incredible number of companies, from here to Santo Domingo."

"Any video production companies or porn films?"

"No, nothing like that. More like land, apartments, buildings, renovation work. The commissioner reckons we're really onto something big."

"When will I get to see your thesis?"

"Tomorrow afternoon, I should think."

The orderly brought round the Corsican parcel at around seven. The day had now started twelve hours ago, after a night that had never really finished. Momo would never benefit from the reduction in the working week. From the packet, he removed a videocassette with neither title nor box. There was no way he was going to watch it there. He might get caught by the head blonde and get another earful.

He got back home exhausted. The shop stank. It was as if the walls were soaked with rain. He fought his way to the TV and the video recorder through the tangled mess on the floor – all sorts of forgotten things, from brown coffee cups to filthy shirts, by way of old unread newspapers. On the screen, there was a scattering of blue snow, a second of darkness, then Elsa in close-up. She was superb, fresh and smiling at the camera, blowing childish kisses with her hand. A little shiver of happiness ran through Maurice. Thanks to the face of the corpse and the photos he'd looked at for so long in her place, he'd ended up knowing the kid. Her face was familiar. At night, he often fell asleep with her, and during the day she was by his side whenever Carla drifted away. He wondered how long ago the film had been made. She looked particularly young, but that might just be down to make-up. She was wearing a large red skirt. Once more Momo pictured the rain-coat on her corpse. Apparently, red was her colour. He slumped down on his bed in his shoes and coat. The girl's movements were slow and calculated. She sat down, looking all innocent, with a thumb in her mouth. She folded one leg, placing her foot against her thigh, level with her buttocks. For a second Momo wondered if she was wearing knickers or if that was the shadow of her sex beneath her raised skirt. She stared slightly upwards at the camera, with a cheeky grin. Then she moved aside her foot, and the flower of her sex appeared, pink and brown beneath the dark hairs. Smiling, she negligently placed a saliva-dampened finger on it, barely touching it then she called out "Karim!" There was no response, so she made some clicking sounds with her mouth, as though encouraging an animal. "Come here, come here!" Momo was beginning to curse the male Lefèvre when a dog appeared. Her dog! The creature her mother never stopped patting! Momo could barely swallow his spit. The kid started caressing the dog, kissing its head, his snout, like something out of *Lassie*, a real hit on the TV, with such a cute girl and such a faithful hound. Then she directed the dog's nose towards the top of her thighs, towards the brown and pink snout of her vagina below its black hairs. "There's a good boy, come on now, come on." Karim's long tongue emerged, slim, agile and rapid, like a dog lapping up water after a run of several miles. You could hear the wet lapping of that large pink tongue on the gleam-ing sex, and Elsa congratulating it and groaning, eyes half shut: "Good dog, there's a good dog." Momo couldn't take any more. He felt all the meals of the day rise up from his guts; meanwhile his penis was hard, reborn, aching. He reached out to press the stop button, got up quickly and put his head under the tap.

Among the crowd in Le Sancerre, which was full to the gills, he tried to calm down. Normally, he never went to this crowded bar. The new trendy Abbesses crowd spilled out onto the pavement around gas heaters. An intense din of chatter mingled with an offbeat unidentifiable music, which didn't seem to reach the ears of the black-clad bikers and cuties. The girls had scarlet mouths and bright colours decking their hair, blue or green maybe, Momo couldn't tell exactly. They were like toys! The whole place stank of dope, and no matter how hard he dragged on his cigarillo, the waves of smoke were getting him stoned at no extra cost. He felt as though he was in the middle of the Sahara, an inhospitable place where there was no chance of meeting anyone, which was precisely what he needed. He was on his third shot of calvados and was starting to see double, but his irritation was still the same, his skin seething and painful, his guts on fire, his penis stiff, and he was savouring that state, which he didn't want to end too soon, to wipe away its last traces straight away with a Kleenex. A girl smiled at him: she had a sad but pretty face and a large nose. She did it again. Momo turned away, knocking down his calvados. He must look like a lunatic, a serial killer. He just had to talk to the male Lefèvre. The cop from Bastia must be getting pissed somewhere between the citadel and Place Saint-Nicolas. Maurice went outside, almost running along Rue des Abbesses to get away from the crush. He got out his mobile, but there was no signal. It reappeared only when he got to the corner of Rue Lepic.

"Of course you woke me up, More is Less! You know full well that I don't have a woman to cook me dinner and put the world to rights. So, in the evening I drink, and wine puts you to sleep. Are you calling to tell me how traumatized you are, or to give me some real news?"

"I was hoping you might be able to add something interesting. Do you think it was Jean-Baptiste behind the camera?"

"Personally, I never think. It's bad for my morale. Anyway, even if he did do the filming, he wasn't the one to have an idea like that in the first place. I can't imagine him persuading a girl like your little sweetheart into doing it. He doesn't have the muscle for it."

"I'd like you to quiz Carla. I have a feeling that she knows about this cassette. Do you reckon you could search her place?"

"Easy does it there. Of course, if I got an official order from Paris, then I'd have no choice. But to be honest with you, round here we're walking on eggs, and I'd rather we thought things through a bit before jumping out of the pan."

"Eggs and pans, I'm fed up with all your kitchen talk, Lefèvre!"

"Our haul is extremely varied: snuff movies, child pornography, plus some amateur stuff like the one featuring your sweetheart. I'll keep you informed. Has my better half seen this masterpiece of the filmmaker's art yet?"

"No, not yet. Even I haven't reached the end. I got a bit sick on the way."

"You're far too sentimental, 'Less than Nothing'. I do hope you didn't miss the shot of your sweetheart's innocent tongue on the fully erect penis of that poor hound."

"Shit! Don't be more of a dog than you are already, Lefèvre!"

"Don't forget your tissues!"

"And what if the kid was murdered because of this tape? That must have occurred to you. If her father came across his daughter doing such a lovely little number, then he'd snuff her to clean the family honour . . . I've already heard of horror stories like that . . . Things that go on in the Middle East! Your Mediterranean tragedies, the code of honour and all that crap! I even once read about a brother who murdered his sister because she'd been raped!"

"I see that little film has got all your hormones jumping, old chap. Of course, the idea occurred to me. But right now, we don't have anything solid to go on. We'll talk again later. Ciao!"

In a fury, Momo pressed the off button on his phone. He felt sick once more. Going up Rue Tholozé, he passed only a few feet away from Elsa's apartment, that dark dank bed-sit facing due north. An anxiety attack gripped his throat, freezing his chest and guts down to his thighs. He practically ran back to his shop, got undressed and dashed into the shower. A huge cudgel was rising up his belly. He clutched at it, as though he wanted to strangle it. At once, his sperm shot out, and it felt as though he was emptying himself out from all his bodily extremities. He stayed there like that for several minutes, motionless in the shower, trembling from the cold, exhaustion and drunkenness.

Still drunk, Maurice carefully dried himself after his shower then combed back his hair. His clean state almost made him look serious. He still hadn't called Anna. It was eleven o'clock, too late, but hearing her voice would do him good and let him get to sleep. He hesitated for a moment, while knocking back two shots of booze.

"It's a bit late, am I disturbing you?"

"Only a public servant could think such a thing."

Maurice took the plunge. He didn't give a damn. He was as tight as Carla's breasts.

"You mentioned giving me a massage. I don't want to insist on the point, but maybe we could have a drink together some time?"

"Personally, I'd prefer the massage. Which doesn't exclude the drink, for that matter. But I only drink Gigondas."

"Fine, Gigondas . . . When?"

"How about in five minutes? That should give you enough time to put on your coat and head up to Rue Lepic."

She was certainly no wallflower. Maurice could hardly believe his receiver.

"Give me a quarter of an hour, so I can put on some trousers."

"Are they that tight?"

"To find some Gigondas. I'll need a moment to think!"

With a clean pair of pants on his backside and damp hair, Momo ran to L'Oracle where Boualem sold him a bottle of Gigondas 1996. Momo now owed him one! He ran back up the stairways and streets that mounted the slope from the Goutte d'Or to the top of Rue Lepic. A marathon, which meant he arrived in a sweat, breathless but calm, his lungs burning so much that any anxiety had been steamed away.

Anna was dressed oddly, in some sort of trendy street clothes, black leather trousers with a jacket over a white T-shirt.

"Some of Manfred's clothes fit me perfectly. We are practically the same size."

He remembered how she spoke about her son in the present tense, as if he hadn't died. In fact, for her, he hadn't. That wasn't how she saw death. With her hair pulled back, she looked a little younger, but Momo still found her old and plain. He thought of Elsa. The image of her smooth smiling face haunted him. A bowl of light caressing his eyes.

"Gigondas 1996, well done! It was worth waiting for. I didn't think you'd find any that fast this late."

"Finding ways and means beyond normal routine is part and parcel of my job."

She opened the bottle with a double-bladed cork-screw, which left the cork intact, then filled two crystal glasses. They clinked. Momo went over to the window. Paris was glistening as far as the lights on the Eiffel Tower and the skyscrapers of La Défense. He couldn't really remember what he was doing there. Just to be away from the mess and dampness of his shop, from Elsa, from work, from himself, with Paris lying at his feet. He was there because he wanted to be with a woman, any one would do, and she was the only one who spoke to him as if he was more than a just a copper, as though from one human being to another. He felt like saying to her: "I need your help, Anna. I need some comfort." But he knew damned well that he wouldn't.

"I was hoping you'd come by," she said.

He didn't dare turn around to look at her. He imagined she was smiling tenderly. He thought of her eyes. He adored them. The rest of her scared him. She wasn't trying in the slightest to be attractive for him, and he'd always vaguely thought that women were there to be attractive. But not her. And yet, even when dressed in Manfred's clothes, there was nothing masculine about her. Her movements were harmonious and light. In fact, such femininity terrified him.

"You have nothing to say?" she insisted, and her voice was soft, even softer than usual.

"As you know, I'm wary."

"You're right to be. The wine's excellent. It should have been decanted. It's a bit of a waste."

He decided to turn around. She'd taken off Manfred's leather jacket; her white T-shirt left her arms naked, revealing their fragile curves. They were beautiful, firm and golden. You could nestle between them, never move again, and that's all he wanted to do: never move again. He refilled his glass, he had an absolute need to be drunk, not to be him, because he could no longer bear that weak-hearted dickless cop whose name was on his ID papers.

"If I give you a massage, you won't need to speak."

"But will you speak to me?"

"That's not the hardest thing. The most difficult part is that you're going to have to undress."

Her face lit up with a mocking grin. Momo wondered if he was blushing or not. He had vaguely sensed a wave of heat rise up from his chest as far as the roots of his hair.

"Then I'll need another drink!"

She filled his glass. He knocked it back in one. The city was still glimmering, and he apologized for having finished the bottle. She handed him a towel.

"You can tie it round your waist."

She left him. As he undressed, he looked at the city lights. He was completely drunk. His nerves had come back, erecting his penis beneath the material, and he felt as if nothing would ever allow him to sleep again. Anna came back holding a bottle. She was calm, as though there was nothing untoward or unusual about what she had just suggested. He followed her into a blue bedroom, where two candles were burning. It was both morbid and sweet. He didn't dare lie down on the bed. He was as nervous as hell.

"Why are you doing this?"

"Because you need comfort, and I can give it to you."

The thought crossed his mind that she was the only person he could trust. But he still had to dare. He would have so liked to have adopted her way of looking at death. He remained standing beside the bed, with the stifling impression of being a condemned man. What she had said at his place came back to him, how the fear of death is simply the fear of dying without having loved or having been loved. The thought made him want to cry.

"Lie down on your stomach," Anna murmured in a barely audible whisper. "And don't be afraid."

It was more than fear: it was inconsolable grief. He got on to the bed. An unbearable weight was pressing down on his chest, an icy hand was strangling his throat and, as soon as his face abandoned itself to the fragrance of the bed, his eyes soaked the sheet. He

118

cried silently. It was the only thing that could do him any good. Then he felt her warm oily hands penetrate his flesh, knead his back, unwind his muscles. He fell into a dreamless picture-less sleep and finally came to rest in the silence of a blue darkness. He was barely aware of being turned over onto his back. He seemed to sense those oily warm hands modelling his arms, torso, thighs, putting them back into shape. At the end of a long clear sleep, he felt a tongue brush against his penis, entwine it, then a mouth engulf it. Elsa haunted him, Elsa and her tender sex, her sweet flower beneath that dog's terrible tongue. Momo heard himself groan. When he opened his eyes, Anna's face was a luminous shell in the waltzing light of the candles. He would have liked his head to empty out. He would have given anything to be alone with her. But how to drop the nightmare of existence, forget the psycho who had killed two youngsters in the Moulin Rouge, Elsa's diabolical machinations, Boualem's Algerian mas- sacres, lunatics capable of ripping a man's throat out with their bare teeth? He put a hand out towards Anna's red flowing hair. Pleasure had illuminated her. Never had a woman made such tender love to him with her mouth. He would never have believed so much sweetness possible. He suddenly hated the rest of life, his job and death, everything that prevented him from being there, quite simply there with her. He mur- mured "you're beautiful". And thought so. She was incredibly beautiful. To love and be loved before dying: it was something he could believe for that sec- ond, and that was enough. Just one second. He touched her round delicate shoulder. He penetrated Elsa's fresh wet sex, her delicate flower. He felt the wave coming, a violent onslaught, several jolts then Anna folding herself around him, drinking him in. In

119

a last burst of remorse, he hoped to make her happy one day, to satisfy her, even if he was completely incapable, and he broke into uncontrolled sobs, snot running from his nose, his throat so tight it was choking him.

He didn't know how much time had passed. Someone was shaking him. He heard himself snoring, he saw her leaning down over him. Anna, and her sparkling eyes. She smiled at him.

"You fell asleep. It's time you went home."

He looked at her in amazement, then brushed his mouth against hers. She was disappointed with him, but not as much as he was with himself. She'd massaged him, sucked him, drunk him, and the idiot had dozed off. How was he going to put up with himself till the day he died?

"When you want love, I'll be waiting for you. Till then, I'd prefer you to go."

With a sleepwalker's gait, shattered, Momo repeated the sentence to himself as he went down towards Rue Gabrielle. "When you want love, I'll be waiting for you." He'd never seen anything crazier than that woman loving him and bringing him comfort. He didn't know how to feel about it. Happiness at having at last met someone. Sadness at having failed to give her the slightest consolation.

When he arrived back in front of the shop on Rue Gabrielle, he noticed that someone was sitting in front of his door. It must be a tramp. He went nearer. It was Rémy, completely out of it and half-asleep.

"Maurice, I've got to talk to you!"

He looked like he did on his off days. Momo let him in. He turned on the light and made some coffee. Rémy poured out some Jack Daniel's. But Momo stuck to a sugarless coffee. He hadn't felt that light for ages.

His despair had vanished. Even Rémy's misery, his face ravaged by drink, his bleary stare, his deformed body, the pathetic way he emptied his glass, couldn't touch him. He thought that one day he would no longer be afraid to die. It was possible, quite possible.

"It's about Malika's nephew," Rémy began. "He's eighteen, and he's got himself involved in some dirty business. His father knocked him about a bit the other day. He just can't take any more!"

"And it's urgent enough to be lying on the pavement in front of my door at two in the morning?"

"Malika's in a terrible state. She's been completely down ever since we lost the baby. Her brother's all the family she's got left. He was the one who took her in when she came over to France, and the nephew's like a child to her. You have to do something, Maurice. Really you do."

Malika was in a bad way, and if Malika was in a bad way, then the oxygen went out of Rémy's life and the blood froze in his veins. Anna would have said: "It isn't my conception of love." Maurice pictured Anna's happy face imprisoning his penis with her mouth. He'd go back to her to love her. He had to. Otherwise, he might as well end it all at once.

"Tell me about it . . ."

"Malika's brother left Algeria in 1975. He works for the police car pound, putting clamps on wheels. He worked hard. Areski's his youngest kid, he was born in France of course, and they spoiled him. But he's turned out bad. I think he's involved in drugs. He works for a cleaning company . . ."

Maurice thought of those Algerian exiles who had arrived in France later on, at the beginning of the 1990s. Runaway victims. And this nephew, born in France, who had fallen into a different nightmare.

"Can I meet this kid?" Momo asked.

"That's what I want you to do. You have to get him out of this shit-hole. But the meeting will have to be discreet. Otherwise, it might be dangerous for him."

Momo smiled. He couldn't help himself, and Rémy thought he was going mad. Maurice dialled Anna's number. Her hoarse tender voice answered at once. Without recognizing his voice, he heard himself say:

"I'll come back just as you said, I promise you that. I just need a little time."

A fine Atlantic drizzle was getting into his bones. Momo was going down Rue Tholozé with his mobile stuck to his ear. He almost felt like some young dickhead who thinks there's an elite and that he's part of it. He could breathe at last. Anna's tender caresses had renovated him. In the distance Paris could hardly be made out beneath its filthy bandages. All that could be seen was the weak glitter of gold leaf on the dome of Les Invalides, like a drawing pin stuck into a wall of tracing paper.

The male Lefèvre was whispering into his ear about his little chat with Carla. The kid had claimed that she didn't know about the tape of Elsa with her pooch, she was even offended that they might think that . . .

"I'm sure you didn't handle her right!" Maurice retorted.

A girl in moonboots turned round abruptly and looked daggers at him. She was fed up of living in a world that had been turned into a phone box. Momo could only agree with her.

"Why, you reckon that bitch would have got her kit off for you?" the fake Corsican sneered.

"You know damned well that I'm not a one for the ladies, even if I am trying to do something about it, Commissioner."

Momo felt sure that Carla would have trusted him. Maybe he was wrong. But being wrong isn't always a mistake.

"Are you going to come back for another whiff of the Corsican shrub?"

"I've got enough on my plate here, Lefèvre. Corsica's not the only place to have fun."

"We actually work over here, and we even get results. One of the lads we arrested in Cap Corse has confessed to buying the master of the dog cassette from your little angel. Six months ago. For twenty thousand francs. Apparently there's a good clientele for amateur films like that. It's the sort of performance that sells for one thousand francs a go. Highly profitable."

"And did she offer him any others?"

"She said that she had more in mind, but he never heard from her again."

"Does he know where it was filmed?"

"That's exactly the sort of thing he didn't want to know. Anyway, he's got no worries. She was an adult, and no one pressed charges."

"Does he know Carla and Jean-Baptiste?"

"No, he doesn't, even though we did grill him like a lamb chop."

"Spare me any more details of your diet. I know you're more into stuffing than savouring. Speak to you soon. And keep me posted!"

Momo strode on, his jaws clamped, a furious expression on his face. So innocence had sold its own innocence? It was enough to turn anyone off from their vision of good and evil. He didn't like that at all. Was Elsa just someone who was coldly calculating about her own career? Was that why she'd been killed? Because she was too headstrong? He grimaced. He still didn't know who the real victim at the Moulin Rouge had been. Elsa or Manfred? The shit-house that was Corsica, the cassette and Elsa's ambitions all made it likely that it was her, and that the pathologist was right.

But Momo refused to believe it. Elsa had gone to Manfred's dressing room to tell him that she was going to become his dresser . . . and had run into the murderer. Yes, that was how he pictured the scene. He even managed sometimes to imagine Elsa back to life again in her north-facing apartment. A red splash on the grey streets, wrapped up in her raincoat, she was running towards that dark workshop, dreaming of Manfred in evening dress. But that vision faded quickly, and all that was left of Elsa was Carla. The young singer would not become a victim of the victim. No matter what the male Lefèvre said, twenty-first century Corsica was not an echo of Ancient Greece. That broad, overly blue sky, that light blinding even the darkest obsessions, the beating of a sea that never slept, polyphonic choirs, ancestral curses, a round of killings that was older than the world itself, all that was just an image. Not a prison. Carla was not going to be a tragic heroine. Momo would do all he could to show that her murdered double had acted alone. The dead girl's blood would never sully her. She had the word of an old goat on it!

He shoved open the door of the workshop-cum-store of the goldsmith-cum-sculptor. A bell tinkled above him. The man with the build of a bodybuilder gave him a cocktail smile: one third surprise, two-thirds pleasure, with a slice of panic.

"OK, Mister Artist, let's get our cards on the table. You were a bit too soft in your description of our little darling, the ex-model. There's a bit of miscasting somewhere. Could you be a little more accurate about her working life?"

"I'm sorry?"

"You're right to be! Because today I'm in one hell of a mood. So out with it, or else I'll send round a troop of useless, extremely clumsy cops to search the place. They'll take their time going through all your stuff, and I won't be able to tell them to handle things carefully. That's not one of their natural qualities. So watch out for yourself!"

The man's eyes fell on his jewels, sculptures, rock crystal, the fine scraps of silver, the tiny lapis lazuli, the brilliant drops of topazes and garnets. He could just picture the mess.

"What do you want to know?"

"If she ever mentioned any photos, or films she was in, and which she wanted to sell."

He hesitated.

"She did ask me if I knew any photographers who were looking for models."

"And did you?"

"I gave her two addresses. Dijon, on Rue Joseph-de-Maistre. And Perotin, on Rue du Chevalier-de-la-Barre."

"And did she see them?"

"I've no idea!"

"Is that all?"

"That's all!"

"Watch yourself. Because I often pass by this way, and I lose my patience extremely easily."

He slammed the door, which tinkled deafeningly. The blacksmith shrank into his apron behind his worktop. Momo took a deep breath; a slight inner laughter shook his diaphragm, a scrap of morning joy that escaped from this greyness. He thought of Anna welcoming him into her mouth. Had he dreamed that? No. That hostage-taking really had happened. He could remember it clearly, and it was still doing him good.

While going down Rue Lepic he phoned Minnie the

little mouse and asked her to check if Elsa Suppini had contacted the two photographers on Rue Joseph-de-Maistre and Rue du Chevalier-de-la-Barre. If so, when? And what had she suggested to them?

"And don't be too polite, be effective. It's urgent! I won't be back to the office till this afternoon. We'll talk around three, OK?"

Giving orders from the street made wings sprout on his back. He flew as far as Rue Constance, then landed by the building where the stage director of the Moulin Rouge had finally returned from Australia.

Susan Penguin was Anglo-Irish, voluptuous and pink in her menopause: slightly aggressive, wrapped up in her woollen pastel house clothes. She'd flown back the previous day and was suffering from jet lag, despite the melatonin – a truly marvellous discovery! Her tiny bijou residence was extremely cosy. Chelsea. Home sweet home. Porcelain cups. But nothing stank of wealth or real-estate investments or diamonds pouring down your neck. The cloakroom attendant who'd described her as so loaded she didn't know what to do with it must have been hallucinating.

"Elsa wasn't a very nice girl. I won't deny that just because she's been killed. She was egocentric, ambitious, and I've no idea if she actually had the talent that could make her succeed. One day she showed me her sketches. I'm no specialist, but I was rather underwhelmed."

"Did you hear about her pornographic activities?"

The director crumbled a scone, then picked up a few pieces of it on her pink-lacquered index finger, slightly dampened with saliva. The finger vanished, its polish matching her lips, into a humid mouth. She shook her head, as though Momo was talking nonsense. He pressed the point:

127

"You know, photos, videos that are a bit . . . hard-core. Apparently she was no wallflower."

"Really?" she said, looking sincerely surprised.

She sipped at her tea, still amazed at the question. Because Elsa had been a serious girl. Dancers and singers might be exposed to that kind of proposition, but her . . .

"You mean they're prostitutes?"

"They work as models, they pose, and sometimes they meet someone. We're delighted when one of our girls makes a good match. It happens, you know."

"That a wealthy customer weds a chorus girl?"

"Yes. But Elsa wasn't on the stage, and she was madly in love with Manfred."

"And he knew that?"

"Of course he did. But he never encouraged her. He was very straightforward. Not a seducer at all. It was as if he came from another dimension. And yet he was our best dancer. Unpretentious, never the diva, always highly professional."

She too was serving him up a perfect Manfred. How annoying! It was hot in this modest apartment. The petals of dried roses were withering in their bowls. There was definitely no reason to believe what the girl at the Moulin Rouge had said about the director's vast means. The walls were lined with books, including a few beautiful old specimens. On a tray, Momo noticed two that had recently been rebound: Carco's *La Rue* and *Pigalle*. He recognized Malika's handiwork. The bindings were a fine honey-yellow, lined with black silk paper on imitation vellum. The flattened skin and grains gave the books clear pure shapes. How did Malika, who was so desperate, so childish, manage to produce work like this?

"Do you have your books bound on Rue Véron?"

"I've known Rémy for ages."

Momo absorbed the bad news without flinching. But he didn't like it. Why hadn't Rémy mentioned Susan to him? After all, it was a link with the Moulin Rouge and Manfred.

"I'm one of Malika's best customers. This is her latest work. She finished them just before I left for Australia, and I haven't put them away yet."

Beside the bookcase, Momo examined a reproduction Utrillo that depicted Rue Saint-Vincent. In fact, it was a canvas, not an imitation, and if it was a fake, then it was an extremely good one.

"Do you know anything about painting? It's a fake, of course, but it's a good illusion."

She'd blurted out this observation, and it seemed to Momo that the tone of her voice was lacking in illusion. He turned towards her. She looked a bit pinker, her lacquered finger in her mouth. He left her to her jet lag, her wilting roses and her fake Utrillo. It was ten-fifteen: he was going to be late for his appointment with Rémy.

Sure enough, his old school pal was waiting for him in his battered Renault 5 on Place Pigalle, just in front of the Chao-Ba. Momo got in the backseat. Rémy was tense as he pulled off.

"I told Areski that I had a job for him. He's short of cash. I was sure he wouldn't say no."

"Why didn't you tell me that you know the stage director of the Moulin Rouge?"

"Because you didn't ask."

"Don't muck about, Rémy. Tell me, is that walking stick of candyfloss rolling in it or not?"

Rémy remained silent, grumbling, not understanding these stupid questions. The silence lasted then he finally admitted yes, he thought so.

"And the Utrillo in her living room, is it genuine?"

Momo sensed that his friend was choking. In the rear-view mirror he studied that once handsome face.

"Well?"

"Yes, it is. And Manfred sold it to her."

Momo remembered how Anna had mentioned a picture that had been sold to help her out when she was ill.

"So that's Philip Leigh's little present. How do you know she bought it from Manfred?"

"As I told you, I met Manfred at the dance school on Rue Coustou. One day he told me about the painting. He needed money. And I knew that Susan was looking for an investment."

"Which would be discreet and paid for in cash, is that it?"

"Yes. I took care of having it valued. It was a good deal for both of them."

"And for you?"

"I got paid a commission. Anyway, I owed Susan. She's a good customer. She's bought some really pricey books from me. And she's given Malika some work. Without her, I'd have been on the street in a second."

Momo went numb. Rémy had lied to him. Was he an old friend or a shapeless memory? Friendship might be possible between a charming young dancer and a wide-eyed lad, but between a wrecked alcoholic and a bitter old cop who stank like an old goat?

"Why didn't you mention all this when I talked to you about Manfred?"

"So as not to create problems for Susan."

"So our sweet British biscuit might have problems? I might start getting interested in her!"

"Here we are. That's him over there."

As arranged, Areski was waiting at the corner of Rue du Poteau and Rue du Ruisseau. Momo lay down on the backseat. Rémy opened the passenger door, and Malika's nephew got in, mumbling something inaudible that was presumably a greeting. Then not a word. The façades of the buildings, the lampposts, the plane trees and the grubby sky started passing behind the windows of the Renault 5. On the ring road Momo sat up. The kid jumped as soon as he touched his shoulder. His eyes were empty, his face aged by wrinkles and drugs, his lips cracked.

"Don't panic, kid, I'm just here for a nice little chat, with no witnesses. Your aunt's worrying herself shitless. And apparently she's right to be. You're mixing with the wrong crowd, which isn't exactly good for your future."

The kid had the traces of burns on the backs of his hands and his jacket. He was completely wrecked by dope: an old man at eighteen. Momo pictured the other one, whose throat had been bitten out.

"How long have you been on the stuff?"

"What are you on about? I don't touch shit like that!"

"By the looks of things, you've seen the dark side of the spoon more than once."

Rémy didn't say a word. He was driving fast around the ring road and Momo started to hope that the poor bugger hadn't drunk too much this time.

"So, let's sum up. You work for a cleaning firm called Propage. You tidy up offices and apartment blocks . . ."

The penny suddenly dropped. A cleaning firm! The mouse had mentioned real estate, renovation . . . which meant cleaning too. That hadn't occurred to him when Rémy had mentioned the kid's job. He'd been too wrapped up in Anna, Elsa and Clara. All those women he'd have so loved to love. But now he was homing in: crack, cleaning, the price of apartments around Abbesses. Dope and real estate. Aline Lefèvre's two hobbyhorses.

"Who sells you the stuff?"

"What's that got to do with you? He's a nutter, your mate."

"Would you rather I cuffed you and took you round the station? It'd be less discreet, but definitely more effective. On the other hand, I don't know what your mates might think about it."

"You've got to get out of this hellhole, Areski," Rémy pleaded. "Come on! Things are going to turn nasty!"

"Fucking mind your own business!"

The kid fell silent, his hands trembling. Anyway, it was obvious he wasn't going to cough just like that.

"You know your aunt's going out of her mind!" Rémy snapped.

Momo cussed. The kid quite obviously didn't give a toss about his aunt or anyone else. All he was thinking about was the geezer who was going to give him his medication, so long as he'd been a good boy.

"Tell me about your job," Momo mumbled. "Do you get to do overtime?"

"We get to clean out other premises sometimes."

"And does eighteen Rue Gerpil ring any bells?"

"No!"

The word shot out of his mouth like a burp. Momo had hit the soft spot.

"Apparently, you've lost your sense of smell. Because this all stinks of shit! Right, so you know the place, and you know that downstairs there's a squat, then a garden and a house at the far side. So what you do is stir the shit up a bit. So as to put the shits so far up the bourgeoisie that they move on and sell fast and cheap. Did you know the guy who had his throat ripped out?"

The kid didn't say a word. But he was quivering like a fridge in motion. He knew about the killing. As a witness, accomplice, the killer? Momo's throat was burning. The most powerless victims, the ones he wanted to protect, all became as guilty as hell. This kid, Elsa, Carla. All those lovely youths were hiding a pile of shit beneath young skins smooth with collagen.

"Rémy, turn off at the next exit!" Maurice yelled. "Then park as soon as you can."

Momo wrenched his jaws open. His nerves were driving his teeth into his jaws. He slapped the back of the kid's head, which released a yell of pain. When the car came to a halt on a supermarket car park, Maurice leaped out, yanked the kid from his seat and slammed him down on the bodywork, hands on the roof. He went through his pockets, found a blade, a small lump of crack and four tiny pearl-like vials, just like the ones found in the pocket of the throat victim. Presumably more of the famous GHB. That dope for fuckers that had given our lady commissioner such bad American memories. In a fury, Momo spun the kid round and grabbed his mouth. Chapped lips began to bleed between his fingers. The kid's teeth were yellow and rotten, his mouth puke-making but lacking any bridge on his left premolars. Maurice threw Areski back into the passenger seat and motioned to Rémy to go on without him. He needed a breath of fresh air. To walk back alone. Riddled with disappointment, Rémy got out and lunged at Momo

"Is that it?"

"No, it definitely isn't. In fact, you should have kept your trap shut. Because if he gets done as an accomplice to murder, then your nephew will certainly not have cheered up his auntie Malika!"

"You really are a bastard!"

"Hang on, you ask me to stick my nose in your crap, and so I do! And now I reckon that your little pal was there or thereabouts when one of his mates got his throat torn out on Rue Gerpil. But maybe that's just the old paranoid pessimist in me talking. When you've been through the wash like I have, everything goes grey. And that's not just because I'm colour-blind!"

Momo went into the boss's office to give her Elsa's cassette, but Aline Lefèvre's face stopped his hand in its tracks. Her voice had the sweetness of a metal saw attacking a particularly tough piece of steel.

"One of the Auvergnat's customers we arrested says that the dancers of the Moulin Rouge take part in rather special parties if the price is right."

"But everyone knows that. It's common knowledge, and there's no law against it."

"But what is less well known is the fact that a certain Rémy Gagnon acts as the go-between. Or pimp, if you prefer. And there is a law against that."

Momo felt an insect buzzing in his breast, and pictured the dampened nail of that pink sugar lump picking up the crumbs from her scone. Susan and Rémy linked together by hard cash, she helping him to scrape by, he finding clients for her flesh pot, she giving work to Malika, he coming up with juicy yet discreet investments – rare books, fine art – so as to launder the cash earned through their pimping. It was an extremely simple business. If a dancer refused to cooperate, then she was easily fired. Momo dumbly clung to his cigarillo to avoid staggering. Aline Lefèvre saw how put out he was, and India ink darkened her eyes.

"You yourself questioned a school friend about the Moulin Rouge case. That's a serious professional fault!"

She was expecting an apology, a confession. But none was forthcoming.

"I've had enough of your pathetic little ways. You can now see damned well that the arrest of the Auvergnat and his customers leads straight back to the Moulin Rouge. The dancers use GHB during their orgies – I've just got the results of your search back. And the pills we found on the girl from Pigall's who you followed the other night are also GHB. The presentation and dosage are different, but they certainly come from the same underground lab as the dope found in the pockets of our throat victim. So maybe there is a trade in sex and drugs behind your double murder."

Momo felt awful. He hadn't mentioned the grey vials he'd confiscated from Areski. Nor would he. He couldn't do that to Rémy. But he did now have to admit that Aline's roundup hadn't been such a lousy idea as all that.

"And what does our chemical sister have to say about all this?"

"She's on the run. She slipped between our fingers, but we'll soon find her."

The girl had been questioned, then released, so long as she remained at the disposal of the police. But she'd apparently preferred to dispose of herself.

Absorbed in her dark thoughts, Aline Lefèvre was looking decidedly stroppy. She was presumably remembering the rape she had suffered in Berkeley, which she was out to avenge here, on the other side of the world, years later.

"Those bloody drugs circulate in this neighbourhood far too easily. But you can count on me to put a stop to that."

She sighed. She was pale, tense and a lot less full of herself than usual.

"I'm leaving for two days. I know that it's hardly the right time; but there's nothing I can do about it."

It didn't even occur to Momo to smile. He knew from Caty that her darling in the Finance Ministry was going to introduce her to her parents. Some sort of official engagement near Chambord. It didn't seem to excite her as much as orgies did.

"Meanwhile, I'm warning you not to inform your little pal about any of this, otherwise I'll open an internal investigation on you . . ."

Momo counted the number of folds in his hand. It was an old hand that was tired of obeying and playing the fool.

"When I get back, I want progress to have been made, both for the Moulin Rouge and Rue Gerpil. Otherwise, the shit's going to really hit the fan! I've had enough of this!"

Maurice sank his head into his shoulders and waited for the storm to pass. It did. He left, still holding the cassette. Too bad. The silly bitch was going to miss out on the exploits of the kid and her pooch.

A ringing phone greeted him in his office. He answered it to hear the fragile hoarse voice of Carla. She was in Paris. She wanted to speak to him. Momo's heart warmed. The kid trusted him, not that wino in Bastia. As he grabbed his jacket, he said to himself that if he kept concealing evidence like this, then he could say goodbye to the force.

He took a taxi to the Bataclan-Café, just by Place de la République. Carla was waiting for him at the back of the bar, her face pale beneath her blue-black hair. She explained to Momo, and only to him because the other cops wouldn't understand, that Elsa had practically forced Jean-Baptiste to lend her his equipment so as to make that terrible videotape.

"Jean-Baptiste had set up a studio. He'd been gradually buying second-hand equipment."

"Helped in part by his protectors in the independence movement, because they too look after their image, I suppose?"

"Of course. He knew people. He knew he could turn a profit."

"And so Elsa asked to borrow his studio?"

"No one could resist her. Jean-Baptiste absolutely adored her. She said she needed money to go to Paris, then find an apartment and a job."

So that was it! Elsa had filmed that scene two years before being killed, that's why she looked so young in it.

"She made the tape all on her own. He just set up the lighting then he left. He didn't even know what she intended to do, and Jean-Baptiste doesn't like that sort of thing . . ."

Momo didn't believe her. But Elsa had been behind the entire project, that much he was sure of. She had been ambitious, unscrupulous and nothing like an angel.

"I'd like to trust you, Carla," he began.

Once more, he savoured that delicious moment when he pronounced her name, as though they could be friends, at least for a moment, just like that, in passing.

" . . . but I think Elsa wanted to show you how far she was ready to go. She needed you and Jean-Baptiste to be involved, and you've never got over it. Ever since, you've stayed side by side, sharing your secret and the insane love you had for her."

Tears ran down Carla's pallid cheeks. Maurice stopped himself from hugging her, even paternally. Yes, it would have done him good to have a girl for a few seconds, because he had no one, not even his father, barely his mother, and he didn't dare think of Anna in terms of someone who really existed.

"She forced me to stay," Carla admitted in a flood of tears. "Jean-Baptiste was working at the time. It lasted all day. I couldn't stand it. The dog couldn't take any more. It was horrible. I just couldn't keep it all to myself. So I told Jean-Baptiste. That's why there was that scene at her place, which the neighbours told you about. Jean-Baptiste was furious. He'd only just got out of prison. He told her that if he got into trouble because of her, then he'd turn nasty. He hated the idea of being taken for a pimp."

Momo thought of Rémy, and a cold shiver ran down his back.

"I won't abandon you, Carla, I promise."

He then explained that Commissioner Lefèvre in Bastia would deal with the case. And that he himself would be informed point by point.

"You're going to have to trust me, Carla. You're going to talk Jean-Baptiste into turning himself in. Then you'll both make statements. The police have arrested the distributors of the cassette. Elsa was an adult, no one has pressed charges, so you won't risk anything. You've both got solid alibis on the day Elsa was murdered. You'll be released at once."

Carla glanced at him in disbelief. She hadn't come all this way to be told that!

"You bastard! You told me I could trust you, and now you want me to turn myself in? You're a real pig!"

"I promise you, Carla. Jean-Baptiste is risking far more by running away from the police. And you must absolutely not put yourself in the same situation."

Momo thought that good deeds weren't his strong suit. Carla, Areski and Rémy, his only childhood friend, who he was now about to drop in it. Not speaking to him was a way of pushing someone like that into suicide – he'd been wrecked physically, was drinking, practically bankrupt, with a wife who was off her trolley. The beautiful singer was right. Inspector Maurice Laice was a real pig. Carla and Jean-Baptiste might fall into the hands of frustrated Corsican policemen or magistrates, who were failing to catch the killers of the Prefect or pick apart the spider's web that held together the French state, the Mafia and the terrorists. And here were two lambs dressed up as scapegoats ready to be burned on the Corsican altar. Carla as one of Sophocles' tragic heroines, caught in the coils of the impossible, cooked in the sauce of destiny, sacrificed to the gods for the death of the girl she looked upon as a sister.

Momo drank his last drop of Desperado. It tasted disgusting. Mister Nice Guy was feeling rotten. And yet, he was doing his best. And he was full of hope! Which for someone as hopeless as him was a bad sign.

He felt as though he was tearing himself away from Carla. He let her run off to her cheap hotel by Porte d'Orléans without even suggesting they had dinner together. He felt too close to her, as though she was a god-daughter destiny had provided for him, and the idea of approaching any nearer to her filled him with dread. His job had taught him to be at the service of the dead, but it was terrible to think that all this time the dead only died to cause problems for the living, who had enough on their plates as it was. Momo would do everything he could to see that Elsa would have to deal with her own death and put up with the solitude of what she had done in her funeral urn. Momo was now advancing towards Elsa's killer with Carla on his shoulders. A Carla who could now sing once more, make the vaults of the porches and churches echo without being afraid of her own shadow.

At the office, Caty the little mouse was still at her desk, a coffee cup covering her nose. She showed him her teeth. He could count them. She seemed to have far more than the average person.

"What about the photographers?" he asked.

"They were a bit reticent, but they were also panicked at the idea that I might start searching through their accounts. I reckon they're bending the rules . . ."

"So?" Momo barked, already accustomed to the girl's bureaucratic obsessions.

"Sure enough, they made stills from Elsa's tape. Each of them paid her three thousand francs for them."

Momo shook his head. Selling animal porn was not really a motive for murder, but it did help get Carla off the hook. Which was more important than anything else.

"I want a report, the photos and signed statements."

"Do I send copies to Bastia?"

"You've taken the words out of my mouth. Otherwise, among the companies that your Pasquier has shares in, do you remember if there's a cleaning firm called Propage?"

He listened to the silence. Caty wasn't even smiling.

"That doesn't ring any bells," she replied.

"Please check. It's really important."

She plunged her head into the icy blue of her computer screen, while he called the male Lefèvre. The fake Corsican was watching a football match on TV to get over his successes, which had rather overexcited him. The rounding-up of a network of porn merchants, whose trade included child porn and snuff movies, was all over the newspapers. It had been an extremely juicy business. Films, videocassettes and Web networks spreading their threads of silk between the USA and Eastern Europe via Corsica and Sicily. There had been nine arrests, ranging from an industrialist in the highest tax bracket and a rheumy member of parliament, the descendant of powerful pimps from the turn of the last century, from an indebted civil servant to a showbiz star with a house by the sea on a private beach that had never been bombed, given the high level of the revolutionary tax he paid.

"So, More is Less, you can stop fretting. The kid's videocassette is a red herring drowned in the Indian Ocean!"

Momo then explained how he had spoken to Carla, and that she and Jean-Baptiste were going to testify.

"There's no need to be heavy-handed with the two of them, Commissioner."

Lefèvre went straight to the point

"I know you're smitten, Less than Zero. You'd better watch yourself! Corsican music is like the song of the Sirens. But don't worry. We'll play it gently. At the service of the community. Like a real advert for the force."

Momo regretted having told Carla to give herself up. But sooner or later, the male Lefèvre and his boys would have found out about Jean-Baptiste's studio and proved that the tape had been made there. Any copper worth his salt, in a less heavily mined context than Corsica, would already have been through the place with a fine-tooth comb.

"You'll also receive a report explaining that Elsa Suppini herself cashed in on some stills of the film in Paris. She really had her head on her shoulders."

"That's not the only place, if certain pictures can be believed."

142

"Don't wind me up, Lefèvre! Everything seems to indicate that she acted alone, and that our two love-birds had nothing to do with it."

"You really think so, or is it just an impression?"

"I really think so. If the two of them get into trouble, then I'll turn stroppy. I'll tell your ex that you still dream of her or something, whatever, I'll drop you in the shit!"

"You know that the arrow does not always reach the target it is aimed at?"

"Is that from the Greek?"

"No, the Latin."

"Good, then with a little effort we'll end up with an Italian comedy. OK? I've had enough tragedy!"

"And so have I. I'm going to head back up north. This big haul means I might get promoted. If I can get a job among the top pen-pushers in Paris, then I'll be able to roger my ex. I reckon that would cheer me up a bit. And I could take you on in my department, More is Less. You're brighter than you look. They ought to call you 'Less is More'!"

"Less is More" hung up, feeling reassured. Carla was going to be OK. He celebrated this new hope by knocking back a shot of bourbon. With Carla off the hook, all the darkness of the Mediterranean would vanish into the whiteness of Elsa's ashes.

He called Anna. The answering machine reproduced Manfred's voice. It was warm, almost joyful; and that voice from beyond the grave, which sounded so full of life, froze his blood.

"There, I think I've found it," the mouse suddenly exclaimed, going pale behind her keyboard.

"I'm all ears."

"OK, Pasquier has no shares in Propage, but a certain Raoul Grave is the majority shareholder. Now,

Raoul Grave could easily be one of Pasquier's aliases. They can be found together in at least five companies. Strangely enough, Raoul Grave also owns three apartments in the building on Rue Gerpil and is on the payroll of the company that employed our throat victim, Hubert Laboureur."

"What about the two apartments Pasquier owns on Rue Gerpil?"

"They're occupied by whores and dealers. The owners of the other apartments are getting so fed up with the situation that they're all selling up. In the past three years, all new acquisitions have been made by private real-estate companies."

"And Pasquier's involved every time?"

"Not always. But we'll have to check out his aliases. They aren't always easy to spot."

Momo sucked at his cigarillo. So maybe Aline Lefèvre had guessed right. Prices were exploding in Abbesses. The neighbourhood was getting younger every day. And so there was cash to be made from the fragile lattice that covered the old quarries of Montmartre. Residents associations could complain all they liked about developers who were bringing home the bacon from a Swiss cheese whose collapse would soon wipe Montmartre off the map. The property market was hotting up around the meringue of the Sacré-Coeur. Montmartre had become a blow out, complete with cheese and pudding.

"Of course, at just a hundred yards from the theatre, in a trendy quarter, with a garden and view over the west of Paris, old man Pasquier is sitting on a gold-mine," Momo grumbled.

The boss was going to be thrilled. Her real-estate fiddle was starting to take shape. Meanwhile she was away bowing and scraping to her in-laws until her back ached. Caty was no longer smiling. But she was still looking proud of herself.

"I dropped into Pasquier's agency, pretending I was looking to buy a place in his building on Rue Germain-Pilon. Because, of course, he's the one who deals with most transactions. He advised me against it, saying that the building was occupied by a bad crowd. Funnily enough, that doesn't seem to put Pasquier off . . . Anyway, it gave me the opportunity to see his mug."

"Smitten, were you?"

"If he was any uglier, we'd have to put him under house arrest."

"That bad?"

"That bad."

"What about the solicitor who takes care of the ground floor on Rue Gerpil, where Laboureur was snuffed?"

"I haven't managed to nab him yet. He's been on holiday this past fortnight. He's coming back in three days."

"Right. In any case, what seems obvious is that via his lawyer and some aliases, Pasquier is acquiring an ever-greater majority holding on Rue Gerpil."

"Precisely!"

It was Momo's turn to smile. In the end, Caty in her office and him on the streets made for a good team. It took all sorts to make a world, and his world was not behind a desk. Being tied to a computer screen, putting together lists would have taken fifteen years off his life. He thanked the mouse.

"You're great, Caty!"

"A giant can see further on the shoulders of a dwarf."

Momo hesitated. Was he being given the role of the giant or the dwarf?

"Though it's a bit uppity of me to think I'm carrying you on my shoulders."

This time, there was a modest, almost normal smile; and the idea of being called a giant made even Maurice's face muscles want to stretch. Was the mouse chatting him up? That hadn't happened to him since he did National Service. Anna must have something to do with it.

"I suppose you've got Pasquier's address?"

"Seventeen Avenue Junot."

"What about Grave?"

"He's registered at Rue Gerpil. But the neighbours say that he's never there. So I'm going to check."

"Good. Well, tomorrow, my little one, you're going to drop your mouse and become a bloodhound. I want you outside 17 Avenue Junot at seven-thirty."

All they had to do was keep tabs on Pasquier. Follow him from a distance. Nice and easy. Momo left the office and mouse, happy to be a poor sod dreaming of earning a smile from Carla.

As he passed by Lamarck-Caulaincourt, he spotted Malika heading up the stairs, a parcel under her arm, looking as ghostly and lost as ever. Momo thought of Rémy and how he still hadn't called round to see him, like the obedient public servant he didn't want to be.

Back home it was terribly cold and damp. He put his oil heater on full blast. Then placed his butt on it while eating tuna straight out of the can. He had a shower, which failed to wash away his fatigue. He hadn't spoken to his mother since Bastia. She answered his call at once, in a clear, almost rejuvenated voice:

"I'm fine, my dear. You really must come down to see me. I've got something to tell you."

"I'm up to my ears right now, so that'll be difficult. What's up?"

146

"I don't really want to talk about it on the phone."

"Please, Mother!"

"I want to introduce you to someone. It's Gabriel. You know, he owns the grocery store on Place de la République."

"Never heard of him."

"I'm going to start all over, Maurice. He's so nice to me. You know, with your father, things weren't always easy."

Momo's throat dried. The mother of a man as ancient as he was still could think of . . . Once again, he pictured the sentence his father had hung over the dresser: "Love is stronger than death."

"So, what do you have to say?"

"Nothing, Mother. But don't worry. I'll be down to see you soon. I promise."

He hung up. This time it was over. Even his mother was abandoning him. He had no one. He was betraying Rémy and dumping Carla. He took several swigs from his bottle of Jack Daniel's, as though he was trying to end up as a dried snake in a bottle of booze. Then he slumped down onto his bed with his camel.

Far away, across the sands, Carla and Anna were smiling at him, tenderly leaning one against the other. He went over to them. His legs sank into the dunes. When he was nearly there, their smiles stretched into bleeding gashes on their faces, and their eyes froze, staring expressionlessly, as though dead. Other wounds opened on their stomachs, large clear cuts from which blood was gushing. From the openings, a terrible shrill noise was pulsating and refusing to go away.

He finally answered the phone, in a sweat. The red numbers on his radio alarm indicated that it was four-thirty. He didn't even have time to be pleased that he'd been rescued from such a nightmare.

"We've got another corpse on our hands, Inspector. And with the commissioner away, apparently it's your job to take care of it."

Momo would have preferred to go back to his horrible dream, but the cop on the line was presumably part of it. Then a terrible idea occurred to him: Carla! They'd called him so he could go and identify Carla!

"Who is it?" he yelled, amazed at having so much energy on waking up.

"A man aged around thirty-five. In a real mess. Just by the funicular at Sacré-Coeur. He's probably a junkie. Shall I call the Drug Squad?"

"Definitely not. Get a medic, I'm on my way."

As he ran towards the scene, Momo's mind was blank. Perched on his shoulders, Carla must be putting her hands over his eyes, like kids do when being carried by their dad.

Motionless and cold as a chill spring morning that refused to arrive, the man had died at the end of a long career. His skin was stretched over his bones, which looked thin and fragile, and his face was covered with burns and bruises. In the light stinking mist that enveloped Paris, the scene resembled the massacre on Rue Gerpil, but this time it was a natural death, so to speak, an overdose of GHB, crack and angel dust. No blood. No bites. Just a dangerous leap and terrible fall. The medic appeared through the yellow smog and started complaining. His wife was on the point of giving birth, and his mind was elsewhere. He confirmed the death.

"Must be an overdose, but he was also given a nasty beating a few days ago. He's covered with bruises."

Momo was smoking quickly to stay awake and forget his early-morning nausea.

"What about his teeth?"

148

The medic remembered the throat job. He opened the corpse's mouth. There was a bridge on the premolars.

"There's a good chance," he murmured.

Momo shook his head. So the murderer had been murdered. The boss wasn't going to be best pleased.

Momo had never enjoyed stakeouts. He lacked the patience. He also needed a lie-in and a cooked breakfast. He had now worked his way through half a box of cigarillos and three sandwiches since the body by the Sacré-Coeur. He'd just had time to draft his report before meeting up with Caty on Avenue Junot at seven-thirty. Since then, he'd been kicking his heels to no purpose.

"Yesterday," Caty said, "I looked for Raoul Grave on our central computer. He's a surgeon who was struck off. Five years back, he was sent down for two years for a professional error he made during an operation that went badly wrong. Here's our man."

She proudly presented Momo with a hazy printout of a photo of a man with brown hair and glasses, his jaws clenched.

"Well done! You're turning into a real cop."

Pasquier lived in a listed 1930s building, made up of what had been artists' studios, each of which must have been worth seven or eight million francs. This haunt of the filthy rich was no longer really Montmartre, more like a millionaire's hideaway, where stars of the stage and screen concealed the multicolour bruises of their multiple face-lifts.

At nine o'clock Pasquier emerged from the building. He was a sweaty fat redhead. Maurice would have preferred him to be less repulsive. He always lost his motivation when the guilty party was this ugly. They followed him to his agency on Rue Lepic. Then the wait started again. Momo and Caty took it in turns to twiddle their thumbs in the car, on the terrace of a café, or in front of the shop windows along the same block as the Moulin Rouge, whose former fire exit could still be seen, topped with a sign of rusty iron. It was hard to imagine that behind these ordinary-looking buildings three hundred people were busying themselves in order to entertain tourists. Pythons, horses, can-can dancers. Beauties from the East or Australia. Pasquier had been so close to the murder in the music hall, but it was too much to imagine that such a tub of lard and cash had been behind the whole thing. Murder, real-estate fiddles, drug dealing, and what else besides?

At ten-thirty Pasquier got behind the wheel of his Laguna, which was parked in front of the agency. Momo pulled off in the 306 to trail him. This carry-on led them all the way to Saint-Ouen, where the Laguna spat out its fat driver in front of a quiet detached house. And the wait started all over again.

An hour later Pasquier re-emerged accompanied by a tall, brown-haired man with glasses, who got into the car with him. It was the struck-off surgeon. Raoul Grave, the ex-con. Maurice handed over the wheel to the mouse and got out. He wandered around the untended garden. There didn't seem to be anyone home. It took him some time to force open one of the ancient windows on the ground floor without causing too much damage. Inside, the atmosphere was dated, with flowery wallpaper and pre-war furniture. There was a whiff of mildew and stale tobacco smoke. The kitchen, den and living room made up the ground floor, and there were two bedrooms upstairs. Nothing to excite the interest of the hacks at *House and Garden*.

The cellar was more interesting. It contained some Bunsen burners, test tubes full of chemicals, heating coils, flasks and fridges. A nice little lab to produce stuff to take you off high in the sky, then crash again before you had time to lower your landing gear. An investigative journalist's dream! Cardboard boxes were full of packets containing the same pearl-grey vials found in the pockets of the throat victim and Areski, while others were filled with the larger grey tabs confiscated from the dancers at the Moulin Rouge, or the junkie who'd now scarpered. More of the famous GHB, the commissioner's obsession. Wearing gloves, Momo slowly sifted through them, took some photos and removed samples. Then he wiped off any trace of his presence. Wasn't Aline Lefèvre going to be pleased that he'd trumped the Drug Squad? She was now going to be able to settle her score.

Momo got a cab to Rue Hermel, the company head-quarters of Propage, where he produced his card and bellowed that he wanted to question Areski, who was apparently out cleaning an apartment on Rue Clignan-court. After another cavalcade and another fit of bellowing, Momo dragged the young Arab into the cab, then into a cell at the station. The kid yelled and dribbled like mad, but Momo warned him that he was now in custody for his own protection, because he had shopped the barracuda who was providing him with his dope.

"What are you talking about? You crazy or what? I dunno the guy!"

"Dunno, dunno . . . no one ever knows anybody . . . The important thing is that our Mister Big knows that you've been arrested!"

Areski gawped at him without understanding. And Momo was in no mood to explain.

"I must apologize for the inspector. He's a bit moody at the moment."

It was Caty, her mouth still full of teeth, who was taking Areski almost affectionately by the arm.

"Don't worry, Inspector. I'm going to have a little chat with Areski. After all, the poor boy has the right to an explanation."

The poor boy! That was certainly pushing it. But a bit of rest wouldn't do him any harm, and if Caty really wanted to play at being Mother Theresa, then he'd let her be as humanitarian as she wanted.

"Inspector, I've left an officer posted outside the agency. You can call him on his mobile."

She handed him the number, then led Areski away. Momo gave his orders to the cop on guard duty. As soon as the fat man returned to Avenue Junot, Momo would arrive with a search warrant and some equipment. Not in the hope of finding anything. It was just to scare him and have the opportunity to bug his phone.

It had started raining again, and Pasquier had just poured himself a gin and tonic when Momo, accompanied by two officers, rang at the door of the listed studio. The inspector told the large estate agent the bad news: he'd been named by a drugs dealer. So now they had to investigate. It was just a formality. The man went white when he saw the warrant. Said it was scandalous. Reminded them how important he was. A big man. Sure enough, he took up quite a lot of room: his pants could barely hold his guts in. Momo contemplated the scene close up. To what trait would he award the prize of ugliness? The watery eyes, the oily scabby pigskin, the bile-green hair, or the fat figure of a Buddha blown up by Islamic extremists? Momo adopted a polite reassuring tone:

"Don't worry, Monsieur Pasquier, we'll be as discreet and quick as we can."

The man forced himself to stay calm. He had to think fast. It was better not to make waves until the storm started in earnest. They went into a huge living room with a glass roof. The rain was tapping delicately on the large metal-framed panes, making a pleasant musical line. Behind the thousands of watery pearls could be seen the yellowish-grey sky. You could slap a four- or five-figure price tag on even the smallest item of furnishing. Momo asked Pasquier to show one of the officers to the bedroom and bathroom. The other cop at once set about bugging the phone. Momo went into the kitchen, where even the fridge was the size of a wardrobe and must have cost as much as a car. It was far too huge for just one man. When you've got too much money, you can't share it. It was something he had to understand. A slice of fortune was already an entire fortune! The interior was very modern, made of glass and burnished steel, with a cunning arrangement of compartments that were set at different temperatures and a machine that produced ice either in cubes or crushed. Momo opened the cheese box, which stank like an organic goat's arse. Even inside the fridge of a man stinking of money, it still smelled of rural France, which was not quite enough to cheer Momo up. In any case, he wasn't looking for anything in particular, just passing the time. He went though the vegetable compartment, then the fruit, before opening a pot of Nutella. Sensimilla! Momo could even cite its *Appelation d'Origine*. It was stuff originally from Mexico, but grown in glasshouses in Amsterdam, then dried electrically. There must have been about three ounces of it there. Not enough to damage Pasquier, but still sufficient to bug him.

In the living room the cop had placed his listening device in the phone and was now pretending to search through a chest of drawers. He made a circle with his thumb and index towards Momo. Pasquier came down his majestic 1920s staircase.

"You've got strange things growing in your fridge," Momo murmured. "The consequences of the greenhouse effect are just incredible! Tropical heat waves in a cooler!"

"Come on now, you're not going to give me your stage policeman's dialogue for just a few ounces of grass! Even the government's now saying that it's less dangerous than booze."

"The policeman is the philosopher's enemy, Monsieur Pasquier. You know our slogan: 'See nothing, hear nothing, record everything.' You'll sign a statement, that's all my down-to-earth copper's brain demands. And don't forget, one pound of a copper's brains weighs far less than a pound of feathers."

The fat man sighed, slumped down onto the sofa and grabbed his gin and tonic.

"I warn you, don't play silly buggers with me. I have connections. You can't just come along and disturb decent people in their homes because some miserable thug has been spouting nonsense!"

He had orange blotches on his hands. It seemed to Momo that his armpits smelled like mutton. It was enough to make you turn vegetarian, to put you off roast pork and lamb for life. Momo lit a cigarillo, gazed around at the room, which was as big as station's waiting hall, with a piglet in its midst. It was a brilliant Surrealist image. The other cop was now coming down from the bathroom.

"I don't think this is tooth powder, Inspector. What do you reckon?"

He handed him a can of cashews. Apparently, the big man was a foody when it came to choosing hiding places. Inside, there were small lumps of grey grimy matter ... like little pebbles. It was crack. Not very much of it either. Not enough to get on the TV news. Pasquier protested. They had planted it in his bathroom. He wanted to call his lawyer. Maurice reassured him politely, humbly. They would just finish searching, he would then sign the statement, and he'd have the rest of the evening to himself. They weren't going to handcuff him, then feed him to the tramps on the straw of a police cell. It was all just part of their investigations. The fat man shut up, poured more gin into his tonic, and Momo sensed a smile creeping up around his cigarillo.

It was a genuine cry of joy that emerged from Aline Lefèvre's painted lips when Momo told her about the short phone call during which Pasquier told Raoul Grave to get rid of any trace of the laboratory in Saint-Ouen. Then Aline Lefèvre's joy erupted even more loudly when Caty told her how, after a two-hour chat with Areski in his cell, she had worked out their system. The crack was distributed via Propage. The cocaine derivative was imported from Santo Domingo concealed in vats of palm oil. The commissioner didn't waste any time on congratulations and instead adopted the tone of an army general in mid campaign:

"We're going to stay here till dawn if we must, but everything's got to be ready for tomorrow morning. Get some beers and pizzas delivered. I'll be expecting you in my office!"

As she tucked into her Margarita, Aline, who was good at speaking with her mouth full, rejoiced at having now attained an overview, a vision worthy of a bonze struck by illumination.

"So, to sum up: our crooked estate agent, Pasquier, invests in property around Abbesses by buying up apartments on the cheap under the cover of various different companies and under various aliases. In order to keep down the prices of some buildings on the borders of Pigalle, he causes a disturbance in the apartments he lets out or whose sale he controls by using a gang of dope-heads, who are delighted to go wild and stir up shit in exchange for their daily medication. To start with, he probably just gave them the crack he imports from Santo Domingo, where, as Caty has learned, he owns several companies that are just as speculative as the ones over here. Then the system got even more lucrative. His friend, Raoul Grave, who had been struck off, is certainly no dole boy. So he suggested to Pasquier that they should set up an underground lab to produce synthetic drugs to pep up the dope-heads' raves. Quite a juicy business. They supplied their little pills to Hubert Laboureur, our throat victim and organizer of raves, who then sold them like hot cakes during the festivities. Unfortunately, our Hubert got a taste for dope, which was his undoing. One day, things turned nasty during a bash on the ground floor of Rue Germain-Pilon. A nutter attacked our techno fan and ripped his throat out. The killer was then given a beating, or maybe even pushed into overdosing. After all, it was necessary to maintain some sort of order in that gang of pill-heads. He died at the foot of the Sacré-Coeur. Thanks to Caty, we now know Pasquier's rather complicated CV, and this leads us to the underground lab. After having his place searched, he tells Grave to get rid of all trace of his cottage industry in Saint-Ouen. And Grave won't have had enough time to do his housework before eight tomorrow morning!"

She stretched, uttering the long cry of a peacock looking for a hen. Maurice was fed up with his cigarillos. His head was on fire, and he hated pizza.

"At eight tomorrow morning we'll separate into three teams. Maurice will head off to Avenue Junot to nab our fat boy. Caty will go round to Propage. Meanwhile we'll keep Areski on ice for his own protection. And I'll go and grab Grave in his chemical residence. Search warrant, samples, the works!"

At five everything was ready. They now had two and a half hours to rest their eyelids. Momo was all-in when he left the office, his eyes burning from two sleepless nights. He'd barely walked ten yards when a hand fell onto his shoulder. It was Rémy.

"You bastard! You really are a shit. The kid's been locked up. I just can't believe it!"

"Maybe you'd rather find him with a blade in his Adam's apple? We're in the process of arresting the entire network that provided him with his dope, and so I decided he should lie low. If he was out on the street, then he might not last the day. It's for his own protection."

Rémy was speechless. He hadn't been expecting that.

"Your nephew was in this shit up to his eyeballs. A fat pig of an estate agent had him under his control."

"Pasquier?"

"How do you know that?"

"Because that bastard owns my shop! It's because of him that I'm closing down. Areski worked for the pig when he turned the shop next to mine into a hairdresser's."

"Sorry, Rémy, but I just don't have time to chat. I have to get at least a couple of hours' sleep."

"You really do think only about yourself!"

158

"How true! And just look at how much you think about other people! When I ask you questions, you tell me everything, nice and clearly, just like an old pal. You even go so far as to tell me that you get paid a commission for providing customers for the dancers of your sweet English biscuit. How nice can you get!"

"Sorry?"

"I'm not supposed to tell you that. They'll accuse me of covering for you, see? If anyone sees me talking to you, then I could really be in the shit."

"I've got to talk to you, Momo!"

"I'll come round and see you about five this afternoon. With the day we've got ahead of us, the cops won't have had time to deal with you by then."

"Don't hold it against me," Rémy muttered, his face ashen.

In the pale light of the streetlamp, Momo saw that he'd been drinking heavily. The athlete he had so admired in his youth was now this wreck. All that remained of his good looks was that blue stare, both soft and sad, bleached by booze. Momo raised a weary hand and walked on. He couldn't take any more.

He was still just as tired at eight, after two hours of agitated sleep, during which his mother gave him a majestic ticking off from behind a grocery till for having dumped Rémy. "You're paid to die, Maurice, even your friend Boualem says so!"

When he got into his unmarked car, with Thompson and Thomson who were accompanying him, it wasn't raining. A new fresh light was gleaming on the façades of the buildings. They parked by Villa Léandre, a hundred and fifty yards away from the listed studio where Pasquier lived.

At the very moment when they'd turned onto

Avenue Junot, Momo had spotted Malika walking along the pavement. She hadn't noticed him. As usual, she was elsewhere, shut up in her world. Grief had sculpted her face. Her nephew's problems must have revived the pain of losing her baby. Momo thought of the massacres in Algeria, and of his father. It was terrible not having enough time to think of the dead. Some day he was going to pay for that.

On Pasquier's landing Alain Bashung could be heard singing: *Malaxe, malaxe, le coeur de l'automate, malaxe, malaxe les omoplates, malaxe le thorax* . . . There was no answer when they rang the bell, even though his car was parked in front of the building. Thompson and Thomson opened the door gently. They were experts when it came to three-point locks. It was enough to make you wonder why cops are such good burglars!

Under the light of the sky pouring through the glass roof, it was hard to tell what Bashung could see that they couldn't: *et du haut de nous deux on a vu, et du haut de nous deux on a vu.* The song came to an end and was replaced by an ad for a supermarket, which made life more beautiful, and then someone started singing the praises of Renault's creativity. Pasquier was still nowhere to be seen in his palace. One of the officers went up to the bathroom. Momo headed for the kitchen, where he found the fat man slumped over the worktop. Beneath the open flannel dressing gown, the huge pink bag had been ripped open round its Adam's apple, a gash from which flowed all the sins of that bread-stuffed pork. The blood, still hot, was drip dripping onto the marble floor. The ceramic tiles on the worktop and walls, the futuristic fridge and the gleaming ovens were splashed with abstract marks, like a huge scarlet Rorschach, in which could be read the

160

craziness and fury of bipeds who failed to forget that basically they were still beasts.

At last Momo was confronted by the link between the Moulin Rouge and the neighbourhood's drug distribution network in that red gash and those stains coloured like fallen maple leaves. The murderer of the couple at the Moulin Rouge had also killed Pasquier, and suddenly everything became incomprehensible once more. Aline Lefèvre's overview of the case did not cover every direction, but only one.

They're not far away from her. Her stomach is trembling. There's nothing she can do about that, it just won't obey her. So her last hour is to be made of this suffering, beneath the corpse of her father, in that mass grave where she is throbbing with pain. What's the point of living now? She's going to open her eyes. She can't help it. That is why she is alive. To open her eyes. And see them: see those who killed while wearing hoods. Faceless cowards. She opens her eyes. She sees the swollen clouds of her tears. Against the sky, one face stands out. She examines its fine features. She carries away that face of a Grecian statue beneath her eyelids. It will stay there forever. She knows why she's going to survive. So as not to forget that face.

Momo had now spent two days discovering corpses. It was a record. He was wiped out, his guts empty and his head full of dynamite. He'd drafted yet another report, calmed down Aline Lefèvre, who had started slapping Raoul Grave around while questioning him. And she should have been happy! Everything fitted. Caty's team had found a pound of crack in the vats of palm oil from Santo Domingo. The mud on the shoes of the throat victim came from the garden in Saint-Ouen, and there was enough dope in the cellar of the house for the story to be mentioned on TV. Raoul Grave would soon be back behind bars, and the Fraud Squad would put its long nose into the crooked co-ownership set-up on Rue Gerpil. Aline planned to search Rémy's place the next morning, convinced that questioning the bookseller would allow them to identify the killer of the couple at the Moulin Rouge. Maurice stared at his shoes. He didn't believe a word of it.

The commissioner was just briefing Agence France Presse when the Drug Squad turned up, furious at not having been briefed at all. Aline Lefèvre became voluble, laying on the insults in large helpings, so Maurice left her to it and went to L'Oracle in a state of semi-coma.

He couldn't remember the last time he'd eaten, but he was incapable of swallowing anything solid. A liquid lunch, then. He ordered some Bordeaux. Boualem picked out a Château Margaux '93 for him, which Momo drank in tiny sips, like a toddler with his pap. Boualem sat down in front of him.

"You'll feel better in a minute."

"It could hardly get worse! I promised Rémy that I'd go round to see him. But what's the point? I can't do anything for him."

"A good lawyer should keep him out of prison, you know."

Boualem then started to sip as well, like a gourmet. Momo couldn't believe his eyes.

"I thought you never drank!"

"Sometimes it would be a sin not to drink."

He said that in a sad desperate tone. Maurice had never seen him look so preoccupied. His hands were trembling. He'd suddenly aged terribly. Momo thought of those bloody images that must assail this former cop without his permission. Butchery, slaughters and massacres storming around his skull. But Momo couldn't do anything about it, not for him, nor for anyone, not even for Rémy.

"Rémy's already in a bad enough state. Getting involved with the police will finish him off."

He poured out some more Bordeaux. It was warming his guts, even if the burden on his chest was not getting any easier to carry.

"I ran into Malika this morning. She looks completely out of it," Boualem said.

Momo had seen her too, and he thought how that poor girl, grieving for her country and for her baby, would certainly top herself if Rémy went down. He tried to picture Carla's face, the way she had trusted him, and Anna's eyes, to which he would never dare return until he had found out who had killed her son. He looked at his watch. Rémy was expecting him, and this was no time for a nice little chat. He stood up, his cigarillo limp between his lips.

When he went into the old bookshop, he was freezing. The place had never seemed so gloomy to him before. It felt like he was entering a tomb. Yet there was still the same smell that he had savoured back in primary school – in other words, several centuries ago. Since that time, how many books were still there on the decrepit shelves, warped under the weight of paper? Dozens? Hundreds?

Rémy came down the spiral staircase, and Momo felt as if death was approaching him. The fear gripping his guts made his smile look even sillier than usual during their routine greeting. He just couldn't help it – anxiety made him look stupid. Rémy accepted a hug with neither a kiss nor warmth. It was awful. Momo wondered if it was possible to stop destiny making you old and ridiculous at the same time.

They sat either side of the tiny counter that acted as a cash desk. The bottle of Jack Daniel's regularly filled up the two thick glass tumblers, with Rémy drinking three or four times faster than Momo. In the feeble light of the shop, between the walls papered with funeral urns, he looked more like a ghost than ever.

"They'll be round with a search warrant at eight tomorrow morning," Momo explained. "Try and get yourself a lawyer as soon as possible."

"Jesus, but I've done nothing wrong. And if it wasn't me, then someone else would have done it! The dancers need a bit of pocket money, and all this goes on between consenting adults!"

"Try to avoid using that kind of argument."

Rémy was drinking his Jack Daniel's like someone lost in the Sahara for three days who has just found water. His eyes were glazed, almost milky.

"When I met Malika, I knew that I'd finally found someone more miserable than me. That's sometimes your only hope – to find something even worse. Malika won't come out of all this alive, you know that, Maurice?"

"It doesn't make any difference whether I know it or not."

"If I go to prison, she's dead."

Rémy was drunk, more than drunk, sick like a true alcoholic reaching his limit. He was speaking with difficulty, his words wrapped up in a thick mist.

"You won't go to prison. I've got some savings. I'll help pay for a good lawyer. And if they won't let you out on bail, I promise I'll look after her."

Our need for consolation is impossible to satisfy.

Momo remembered the title of a tiny book that Stig Dagerman had written just before committing suicide. Yes, it was impossible to satisfy. Momo would have so liked to console the only real friend he'd ever had, but between desire and reality there is always a gap. Putting up with the same dickhead from birth to death is the torment of everyone's existence, divorce being forbidden and suicide final. Maurice had never before found cohabitation with the old goat he had become so unbearable as he now did.

"With her, I was back in the dance. The way she beautified books was a sign. The grace of her movements when she works, when she strokes the leather, her patience, her skill."

Rémy staggered over to Malika's workbench in the storeroom. He fiddled with the blades, gouges and stylets which had been carefully tidied away beside the leather and marbled paper. Before these sharp tools, skins of dead animals and the writings of people who had been buried for decades and were now mere bags of dust Momo felt as dead as all the corpses he had recently been bending over: his father, Elsa, Manfred, the dealer, the body by the Sacré-Coeur, Pasquier . . .

"You shouldn't pester Maurice, Rémy. It's not his fault."

Malika was coming down the spiral staircase, wearing a short sleeveless dress, her heavy brown curls dancing on her shoulders. She looked like a little girl. Momo thought of Anna, the redhead whose eyes he was now looking forward to, despite himself, as though he needed them to see clearly.

"I don't want Rémy to pay for me. I recognized Manfred. I'd transported his face inside me. During all those years, all I'd done was to keep that face with me, so that some day I could recognize it."

Momo felt a dagger stab into his guts. He remembered Boualem's tale, the horrors of Algeria, the exiles who still look round in the street in fear of recognizing a killer. The tragedy the male Lefèvre had talked about, that terrible fratricide, all that vengeance all those massacres beneath the infinitely blue Mediterranean sky, it was over there, in Algeria, on the other side of the sea, that it had all happened. It was there where the terrible goat song could be heard.

"Shut up, Malika, please!"

Rémy swayed over towards her and wrapped his arms round her shoulders. In fact, he was too drunk to stand and was hanging on to her, while Malika continued her lament.

"I recognized him, so I had to kill him. I thought I had time, but I was wrong, because the baby died! I had no more choice, I had to act quickly, before he started spreading evil around him."

Momo couldn't breath. So Malika had killed Manfred, the handsome dancer, the perfect son, the faithful lover, because he looked like some mad killer in the Algerian bloodbath? Right from the start, Anna had thought it had been some terrible mistake, and she was right. Momo trembled. He thought of *Pierrot le Fou*, and the tragicomedy of existence. He missed Anna, he would have liked to go to the sea with her, to make love on the beach. Forget everything between the earth, sea and sky. Play at living fast so as to die beautifully, like Ferdinand in Godard's film.

"Be quiet, Malika. Manfred had nothing to do with all that!"

Rémy was an old man, slumped in a chair. Words, puffed up with alcohol, started bursting from his mouth, in a sombre litany that he must have recited thousands and thousands of times:

"Her entire family was massacred in a village in Algeria seven years ago. She was saved by her father, who died on top of her, soaking her with his blood, so they thought she was dead. She saw one of the men with his mask off. And she's sure it was Manfred, but he was in the USA at the time. I have proof of that. I spent entire nights telling her that it just wasn't possible, that Manfred had nothing to do with Algeria, but she wouldn't believe me! When the baby died, she didn't say anything to me, but she thought that if she didn't kill the person responsible for the slaughter of her father and her family, then she'd pay for that all her life. Then she quietly prepared the killing . . . It's terrible, Maurice. What could I do, later on, when I found out?"

"I didn't mean to kill the little sewing girl. But she saw me, and she was going to take away my face with her, just as I'd done with the monster."

Momo had a rotten taste in his mouth. He pictured Malika going into the Moulin Rouge to deliver the director's books before she left for Australia. Everyone knew her, so no one noticed her. She bumped into Manfred then followed him to his dressing room.

"Yesterday, I told her what you'd said to me about Pasquier, Maurice . . . but I would never have thought that she'd have gone to his place and then . . . She wanted to save Areski, to save the shop . . . I had no idea."

Maurice should have had an idea. He'd bumped into Malika just beside Pasquier's place. So that was it. She'd rung his bell early that morning, spoken to him, blade in hand, insulted him for all the evil he was doing to Areski and Rémy, by doping her nephew and driving her husband out of his shop. Then she'd bled him, like Manfred in his dressing room, so that justice would be done.

Momo got to his feet. He needed air. He felt like burning all those dusty old books that were weighing down on him. What he'd imagined he would feel when faced with the murderer that day when he'd first seen Elsa's body hit him at last: infinite sadness and despair . . .

"She's not responsible for her actions, Maurice. Can you imagine what it must feel like having your father's body lying on you for hours on end?"

No, Maurice couldn't really imagine that. But nor could he extricate himself from that nightmare. The interlacing of bodies. How had this woman, who was emptied of all being, discovered the strength and cool-headedness in her desperate madness to shift the corpses and join them together in that obscene embrace? By sheer craziness. She'd put them together to recompose the scene she had lived through, beneath the still-warm and bloody body of her father seven years before. To stage that unbearable memory

171

and so wipe it out, to break the spell, to take away the evil that had massacred her family, then her baby . . . Manfred – handsome, mysterious Manfred – looked like one of her torturers. Her madness had believed it . . .

"She isn't responsible, Maurice!"

Momo looked at the two ghosts standing in front of him. He had never felt so old and powerless. His eyes were burning, tears were about to pour out. He had to see Anna at once.

The police would come the next day, so he could grant Rémy and Malika one last night of their bad dream. By going over and over such horrors, they must have succeeded in finding some moments of light. He hugged Rémy. Tenderly. With love. A tiny love that had never succeeded in growing within him, a bud that had never blossomed.

"I'll be there with the police tomorrow morning. You can count on me. I won't let you down."

It was eight in the evening. Outside, as he walked up towards Rue des Abbesses, Momo phoned Anna in Beauvais. He could be there in an hour. She would be expecting him.

At L'Oracle, everything was in motion. Boualem's face fell when he saw him come in. Momo could barely hear himself mutter:

"You knew about Malika?"

Boualem stared at him in terror, silently. Then he started speaking in snatches:

"Deductions . . . suppositions . . . it's hard to stop being a cop, you know that! I saw Malika the day of the Moulin Rouge killings. She was out of her mind. She said that she couldn't have done otherwise. I knew that she was looking everywhere for the man she'd seen during the massacre in her village. When I read

172

the article in *Le Monde* about the murder, then the idea did cross my mind, but I didn't want to believe it, you understand, it was crazy, ridiculous ... that dancer had nothing to do with us ... So I stopped thinking about it. I don't want to be a policeman again. Ever!"

He preferred to stick to his recipes and classy wines. Remain at the oral stage and think that existence is just a bottle you suck.

"Why didn't you tell me?"

"Earlier on, I tried. But you weren't listening to me."

Momo didn't reply. The old goat was deaf, in fact; that was why he sang off key.

"Yesterday, what with that business with Pasquier, I had a terrible premonition ... As I told you, I bumped into Malika."

"I know. So did I. But by then it was too late. I need your car, Boualem. Right now. I'll bring it back tomorrow."

Momo was driving like a madman, sniffing back his snot. He was trying to picture Anna's eyes, but they had vanished. They alone could give him back the courage to live in this diarrhoea that was surrounding him constantly. Lefèvre had been right. Tragedy engendered tragedy, victims led to more victims. Mankind's insanity was in constant need of a scapegoat. And Momo no longer wanted to watch the show. His only hope now was that Carla would get off the hook, and that she'd burn her magical voice onto a large number of albums. And that Anna would once more offer him her eyes.

He got lost in the suburbs of Beauvais and called Anna for help twice on his mobile. When he arrived in the courtyard, he ran over to an illumined building. It was her workshop. As soon as he opened the door, he was flooded by violent light, engulfed in hell fire. With bare arms, wearing old trousers cut off at the knees, Anna was blowing into a rod, slowly inflating a ball of fire into a transparent bubble of light. Momo thought that it was just like this that she had removed him from hell, to enlighten him and blow life into him. Her hair shone in the glow from the furnace. She didn't look like a woman, she was far from the sleek brunettes of his dreams, and it was precisely for that reason that he loved her. She was much more than a woman: she was the entire world, handling the earth, air, water and fire. She plunged the tender glass into a tub, causing pure steam to rise up, then she went over to Momo and pulled him against her. Their tongues searched for each other, licking, while their hands rummaged and undressed. On the floor, sweat made them slide on top of one another, Momo didn't even wonder if he had an erection, if he had a penis, what he should do, he knew what she wanted, her entire body was telling him, word for word, it was enough just to pay heed to each inter-jection that her skin, her hands and her mouth uttered. It was when he heard her purring in orgasm that he melted into her, and they stayed there for a long time, exhausted, covered with water. Momo was warm at last.

Anna laid a blanket on the floor, they rolled onto it, and he put his mouth to her sex for a long time, the crackling of the fire mingled with her groans and sighs, and it seemed to Momo that he was going finally to forget those intertwined corpses, death and blood. All he could hear was Anna's voice:

"You lick marvellously, my love. And that's the best thing in the world."

When he left at seven the next morning, she didn't protest.

174

"The day when you really want me to be with you, I'll be there."

On the motorway in the clear morning light Momo knew that he was returning to the night even though he had just seen the day dawn for the first time. How had he found the strength to leave Anna? He was heading towards Rémy's misfortune, which was also his own. A shared disaster. As for Anna's happiness, that belonged to another world. He would never be strong enough to be as alive as she was. Even if her eyes remained windows wide open on the soft sun that was caressing his skin.

When he stopped for petrol in Senlis, he thought it must have been her who had traced this poem on the filthy walls of the toilet, as a message to him:

your sex
speaks
my tongue
search me
make
of me your garden
console me
for only being
half of you

Toilet graffiti as a sign of hope! Momo thought that he didn't deserve any better. He hadn't even been capable of telling Anna who had killed her son. How could she trust such a coward?

In Montmartre he panicked when he saw an ambulance and two police cars blocking the entrance to Rue Véron in front of the second-hand bookshop. Uniformed officers were chasing away the curious. He elbowed his way through and leaped up the spiral staircase. Forms were busying themselves around a mattress on the floor. Rémy and Malika were smiling like angels, intertwined in love. A double suicide after the final day of their nightmare. A mirror image of the double murder at the Moulin Rouge, itself the reflection of a massacre in a village in Algeria. Momo started sobbing like a little girl, silently, his elbows bent over his stomach. *Our need for consolation is impossible to satisfy.* Anna wasn't strong enough to help him to survive this slaughter. Love and death always ended up screwing together to engender the goat song. Before Anna, the only girl who had ever consoled him had died in his arms, killed by a defective water heater. Snot and tears were eating into his face. He ran away.

In the street, doubled up, arms over his guts, he staggered, hit by an incurable woe. He might as well stop pretending and face up to the fact that he was nothing but an old wreck. He thought of Anna's promise: "The day when you really want me to be with you, I'll be there." He would have so liked to have loved her again. Not to wait for death before holding her against him. Tell her about the terrible mistake that had led a victim to murder her son. Then forget with her. But he couldn't destroy that dream. Fear would always paralyse him. Anna was too much alive for him. He didn't deserve her. She'd made him believe that he hadn't completely had it, that he could still love and be loved. But that was meaningless. He sensed a stare burning into his neck. Was it her? No, it couldn't be her. He refused to hope for that. He stopped himself from turning around.